Racing Home

Racing Home

ADELE DUECK

COTEAU
BOOKS
FOR KIDS

www.coteaubooks.com

Edited by Barbara Sapergia
Design by Tania Craan
Typeset by Susan Buck

Printed and bound in Canada at Gauvin Press

Library and Archives Canada Cataloguing in Publication

Dueck, Adele, 1955-
    Racing home / Adele Dueck.

ISBN 978-1-55050-450-7

    1. Frontier and pioneer life--Saskatchewan--Juvenile fiction.
I. Title.

PS8557.U28127R33 2011   jC813'.54   C2010-907542-0

Library of Congress Control Number: 2011921831

2517 Victoria Avenue
Regina, Saskatchewan
Canada   S4P 0T2
www.coteaubooks.com

10 9 8 7 6 5 4 3

Available in Canada from:
Publishers Group Canada
2440 Viking Way
Richmond, British Columbia
Canada   V6V 1N2

Available in the US from:
Orca Book Publishers
www.orcabook.com
1-800-210-5277

Coteau Books gratefully acknowledges the financial support of its publishing program by: the Saskatchewan Arts Board, the Canada Council for the Arts, the Government of Canada through the Canada Book Fund and the City of Regina Arts Commission.

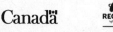

To my husband, Raymond,
who supports me in every way.

Table of Contents

CHAPTER ONE – June 1908

Flat Land

Erik stormed out of the general store, letting the door slam behind him.

Lars Hanson wasn't here!

They'd come all the way from Norway to find his step-father's brother, but he was never where he should be.

Stepping into the street was like walking into a sauna. Erik wiped the sweat from his face, wishing he could get back on the train and leave the dusty grey town far behind. He wanted to yell or throw things. He wanted to tell his stepfather how stupid it was to travel thousands of kilometres to see someone who wasn't there.

Mostly he wanted to ask his mother why she'd married Rolf Hanson. Erik was twelve; he was sure he could have supported the family. She hadn't needed to marry just to get a home.

She'd told Erik they'd live in Rolf's house in the village and he could go to his grandparents' farm whenever he wanted.

Instead Rolf had moved the whole family to America.

"Erik! Erik!"

Shading his eyes from the hot sun, Erik saw his sister

running toward him, her shoes pounding the boardwalk, her long, almost-white braids flying behind her.

"What's wrong, Elsa?"

"Mama fainted," exclaimed Elsa. "I heard someone fall and people yell. When I turned around Mama was on the ground."

"What do you mean? Weren't you with her?" Erik grabbed Elsa's hand and started running.

"I was sitting beside some people speaking English. I was trying to see if I could understand them –"

"You were supposed to stay with her."

"I wasn't far –"

"Where is she now? Is she hurt?"

"I don't think so. A lady helped her to the bench and brought water." Elsa hardly had breath to speak. "Mama didn't say, but I knew she'd want me to get you and –"

"Don't call him Papa!" Erik interrupted.

"I didn't," Elsa protested. "Where is he? Where's –" There was the smallest of pauses. "Where's Rolf? Mama will want him, too."

"In a store," Erik said, pulling her along.

"Should I go back for him?" Elsa tried to free herself but Erik didn't loosen his grip.

"He knows where Ma is. He'll come when he's ready."

When they reached the train, Erik saw that people had begun unloading their settlers' cars, piling belongings everywhere. He dropped Elsa's hand as he scanned the crowd.

"He'll be worried." Elsa glared at Erik before marching away.

Erik wasn't sure that Rolf would care, not that he knew what Rolf thought about anything. Erik didn't talk to Rolf, and Rolf didn't talk to Erik.

Rolf had married Erik's mother in October, 1907. In March, 1908, they'd crossed the ocean to New York, then gone on to Minnesota to meet his brother.

Only Lars wasn't there. He'd left a message about going to a town called Hanley, in Saskatchewan. After three months in Minnesota, they loaded all their belongings in a train and headed north.

Now they were in Hanley and Lars was gone again.

Through a gap in the crowd, Erik saw his mother on a bench. A woman in a dull green dress sat beside her, patting her hand.

"Ma! Are you all right?" he asked when he reached her. "What happened?"

"I'm just tired," she said. "I didn't know a train ride could be so difficult."

"It was terrible!" exclaimed the other woman in Norwegian. "Two weeks we were on that train, what with all the stopping and waiting. It's no wonder you fainted, you poor dear, and in your condition, too."

Erik shot the woman a sharp look. *What condition?*

"Where is Rolf?" Erik's mother, Inga, asked hurriedly. "I thought you were together."

"We were," said Erik, "but he was talking to a store-keeper. I was outside the store when Elsa came."

"He wouldn't let me get Papa," Elsa added indignantly.

"Did he find Lars?" Inga asked. "Was it his store?"

"He's not here," said Erik. The minute the words

were out of his mouth he regretted them. He should have let Rolf tell her his brother had let them down again.

"Not here?" repeated Inga. She pressed her free hand to her forehead.

"Rolf will explain," said Erik. He moved away, watching a man leading horses out of a boxcar. Erik wished they had a team like that instead of Rolf's clumsy oxen.

"Inga, I found him!" Hearing Rolf's voice, Erik came back to the platform. "I found Lars."

Inga's eyes met Erik's for a moment, her lips pressed together firmly, but when she turned to Rolf she was smiling.

"That's wonderful. Do they live here in town? Did you see Kirsten and –" There was a slight hesitation. "And Olaf, too?"

"Well, no," Rolf said, rubbing his thick red beard. "I didn't see any of them. But," he added more quickly, "I know where they are. They've moved to a new town just a short distance away."

Erik stifled a groan. *So much for finding Lars.*

"He and his partner own a lumberyard here," Rolf went on, "and they're going to build one in the new town. His partner, Gunnar Haugen, invited us for supper and to stay the night."

"Ma fainted," said Erik, watching Rolf's smile disappear. "She can't walk far."

"Inga, are you all right?" asked Rolf, dropping to one knee beside her. "Should I find a doctor?" He glanced around. "There must be one in a town this size."

"No, no," said Inga.

"Or a buggy? Maybe someone can give you a ride to the Haugens' place."

"I was tired. I'm not used to the heat yet. If I take your arm, I'll be fine."

"First I must speak to the station agent," said Rolf. "We'll unload the car after we eat."

The animals should be unloaded now, Erik thought. The cow and oxen needed to walk. They'd been fed and watered, but they'd be weak from not moving for so long.

Rolf was back in a moment. "There's no hurry," he said. "The train doesn't leave till tomorrow."

"Did he speak Norwegian?" asked Elsa.

"No, but my bit of English seemed to work." He tugged on one of Elsa's braids. "Did you think I'd need you to translate?"

Erik followed slowly as Elsa skipped along beside Rolf and Inga. None of them, not even his mother, glanced back to see if he was coming.

Someone bumped into Erik from behind, almost knocking him over. "Get out of the way, kid!"

Erik stumbled, glimpsing pointed-toed boots and wide-brimmed hats. Cowboys! As the two men stepped into a building, one glanced over his shoulder at Erik, revealing a sour face and a drooping black moustache. Through the open door, Erik saw other men sitting at tables, drinking and playing cards.

A moment later, Elsa dropped back beside Erik. "It doesn't look anything like Norway, does it?" she said.

Erik glanced at the grey buildings lining the dusty

ADELE DUECK

street. There was nothing behind them but blue sky and prairie.

"No," he said shortly. "It doesn't look anything like Norway."

He wished he was still on his grandfather's farm, not here in this flat land with its unpronounceable name. He missed the mountains and the trees. Even Minnesota was better than this. At least there were hills there. The part of Saskatchewan he'd seen was barren and empty. Only someone who knew nothing about farming would think he could farm here. Someone like his stepfather, who'd never ploughed a field in his life.

Rolf stopped beside one of the unpainted buildings.

"This is the store Lars owns with Gunnar Haugen," he said. He led them around the side of the building past piles of lumber and poles. The door opened just as Rolf lifted his hand to knock. A man stepped outside, stopping suddenly when he saw them.

"Ah, Rolf Hanson!" he exclaimed in a deep, booming voice. "You're here quickly. This must be your wife." He held out his hand to Inga and then to Elsa and Erik. Eric saw his mother wince when he grasped her hand. When his turn came, he realized why. He wondered if Gunnar Haugen had broken anyone's bones while shaking hands.

"I'm sorry that Lars and Kirsten aren't here to greet you," he said, still speaking Norwegian. He stuck his head into the room behind him. "Luise," he bellowed, adding in English, "Come out here!"

"I don't know how good your English is yet," he said, switching back to Norwegian. "But Luise, my wife, she

6

speaks German. No Norwegian at all, so I don't use it around her. She doesn't talk German to me, either – except when she's angry, of course." He laughed as his wife joined them.

"Come in, come in," she said. "Do not stay outside."

The smell of food surrounded them as they stepped into the kitchen. After days of flatbread and *gjetost,* Erik was excited to have a real meal again.

The table was set with bowls and mugs. Mrs. Haugen pointed to a bench for Elsa and Erik, then gave chairs to Inga and Rolf. Mr. Haugen pulled up a chair for himself, still talking. It was English with just a word of Norwegian here and there. His English was simple enough that Erik knew he'd heard most of the words before, but he had to think hard to remember what they meant.

Mr. Haugen stopped in the middle of a sentence, switching suddenly to Norwegian. "You're too tired to think English today," he said. "I'll quickly tell you in Norwegian, then we'll go back to easy words in English."

Erik nodded with relief, and saw his mother smile.

"This new town is just thirty-five miles away." That was fifty-six kilometres, Erik calculated. He'd learned in Minnesota that people measured in miles here, but he was used to the metric system from Norway. "There's no train yet," Gunnar Haugen continued, "but they're working on it. The town will be named Green Valley because of the trees between it and the river."

Erik's ears perked up at the mention of trees.

"Right now it's a wheat field," said Mr. Haugen, "but Lars and I decided not to wait till they auction off the lots. Earlier this spring we built a small building a couple of miles northeast of where the town is going to be. Lars and Kirsten live in the building, and we're hauling as much lumber there as we can. That boy of his has been a big help. Works like a man, hauling as fast as the train brings it to Hanley."

Mr. Haugen stopped speaking as his wife dished out soup with a large metal ladle. Erik's first spoonful told him it tasted as good as it smelled. Along with the bacon-flavoured cabbage soup were thick slices of fresh white bread. It seemed strange to eat soft bread when it wasn't Christmas or Easter, but Erik didn't complain. He declined the *gjetost*, though. He didn't want to eat the brown goat cheese again for at least a year.

"They'll have the big auction sale in August," Mr. Haugen went on. "We'll buy a couple of lots and, since the building is on skids, we can move it to town that very day."

Mrs. Haugen offered cake, but both men shook their heads. "We must unload our car," Rolf said in Norwegian, with Mr. Haugen repeating the words in English. Erik watched Mrs. Haugen put the cake back on the shelf. She caught his eye and smiled.

"Later," she said. "Before bed, we have cake."

Erik nodded, embarrassed, and followed the men out of the kitchen.

"Wait for me," called Elsa from behind them. "I'm coming, too."

"You can't unload the train car," said Erik. "You're too little."

"I can unload as well as you," said Elsa, tossing her

head so her braids danced. "I'm nine years old."

"You'll be a big help," said Rolf, holding a hand out to Elsa. "I'm glad you're coming."

When they reached the train, they saw some settlers loading belongings onto wagons, while others were making piles beside the tracks. One family had finished emptying their car and was spreading canvas over the pile.

Rolf opened the door to the car. The cow and the two oxen turned their heads, and the cow lowed.

"Time to get out," said Erik, pulling himself up into the car. While the men placed the ramp in the doorway, Erik untied Tess and turned her around. "No more trains for you," he said as he encouraged her toward the ramp. "From now on you'll have to walk."

Erik doubted the cow wanted to walk all the way to Green Valley. But, like Erik, she didn't have a choice.

CHAPTER TWO

Closer

Elsa stood at the bottom of the ramp with a fistful of grass. "Come on, Tess," she coaxed. "Come get the good grass."

Tess headed straight down, her head stretching toward the green blades in Elsa's hand.

The oxen, Black and Socks, were soon tethered near her in the grass by the train track. Erik lugged the crate of chickens over beside them. One of the brown hens lay stretched out on the bottom of the cage, while the others walked on top of it. He reached in for the sick chicken, dropping her on the ground. She twitched slightly. Shrugging, Erik gave water to the healthy hens while Elsa filled their food dish. He went back to the car for another load, but Elsa stayed with the hens, trying to get the sick one to drink.

Near the track they piled the chests and boxes of household supplies brought all the way from Norway, along with the few pieces of furniture they'd purchased in Minnesota.

Very carefully, Rolf carried out two panes of glass. They were wrapped in a quilt, then slid between pieces of wood.

"Windows," said Rolf proudly, "for our new house."

Erik tipped over the water barrel, letting the last of the water spill onto the floor of the car before rolling it down the ramp. The other water barrel, heavy with pails, hand tools and a rifle, had to be moved more carefully.

As they worked, Erik watched enviously as another family led out six horses, two cows and some pigs. Turning away, he shrugged his shoulders. At least he'd only had to care for three animals on the train, not twelve.

Mr. Haugen and Rolf half-carried, half-dragged the walking plough. Erik and Elsa brought out stovepipes and tarpaper. Almost invisible against the wall of the boxcar, Erik saw his skis.

The last thing out of the car was the wagon. As soon as they set it upright and tightened the wheels, Rolf said they would fill it.

Erik felt his eyebrows shoot up. *Now? It's almost dark.*

"Good thing I came," said Elsa. She ran over and grabbed the handle of one of the round-top trunks. "Can we put this in first?" she asked.

"Possibly," said Rolf. He glanced at the pile of belongings. "Yes, I think so."

Loading the wagon took longer than unloading the car. Everything had to be packed carefully to make it fit. In the end there were a few pieces left by the track.

On top of everything was the crate of chickens. Elsa carried the sick hen in her arms, cradled like a baby.

"She drank some water," she told Erik. "I think she's going to live."

Back at the house, Mrs. Haugen served large pieces of

rhubarb cake while Inga struggled to describe the rhubarb soup she'd made in Norway.

When the cake dish was empty, Erik wrapped himself in a blanket on the kitchen floor, glad to be in a house after sleeping so many nights in the train car with the animals.

The sound of coals being shaken in the stove woke him in the morning.

"Ready for breakfast?" Mr. Haugen asked in English. Erik nodded and watched him lay thick slices of bacon in a black frying pan.

Mrs. Haugen took bread and coffee to Erik's mother in the bedroom. Elsa helped with the dishes while Erik went outside to water the cattle.

He was just finished when Rolf and Mr. Hanson drove up in a wagon drawn by two immense black horses.

"Beautiful," Erik breathed. "As good as grandfather's horses."

Mr. Haugen climbed down from the wagon. "Beautiful they are," he agreed, slapping the nearest horse on its flank, releasing a small cloud of dust. "Too bad they aren't mine."

"Not yours?" asked Erik.

"No, Olaf has my team hauling lumber to Green Valley. I borrowed these so we could get the last of your belongings."

While they spoke, Rolf climbed over the wagon seat and tugged a chest to the edge of the box. Gunnar Haugen grabbed one end and Erik the other. Piece by piece, they stowed everything in a corner of Mr. Haugen's stable.

After they added his mother's sewing machine to the pile, Erik saw Rolf loosening the rope holding the canvas cover on their own wagon. "We'll take out a few things," he said to Erik. "Elsa and your mother are staying here while you and I join Lars."

Erik stared at him. *Staying? While he and Rolf joined Lars?*

"Inga is tired," said Rolf. Not looking at Erik, he pulled the corner of the canvas back. "Mrs. Haugen will look after her while we find a place to live. Maybe Lars has already found us land."

And maybe there will be a house and furniture and a money tree growing in the garden.

Erik bit his lip hard. His mind pounded with questions, but instead of asking them, he nodded and helped Rolf wrestle a box from the wagon. When he carried it into the house, Elsa met him at the door. "I'm to stay here with Mama," she said. "Mama is sick, I can tell. And Mrs. Haugen doesn't speak Norwegian. What will I do?"

"You know some English," Erik said. His voice was rough. "And Mr. Haugen speaks Norwegian."

"Yes, but he –" She stopped suddenly as Mrs. Haugen came into the room, speaking quickly. Erik stood, still holding the box, staring at her. She gestured to the corner, speaking more slowly. It was English this time, and Erik realized the first words had been German. He could see why Elsa was afraid.

He put the box against the wall, under the bench. When he turned to go back outside, he heard his mother call his name.

"*Ja, Mor,*" Erik replied, stepping into the bedroom. She lay against a pillow, her brown hair, the same shade as Erik's, loose around her face. "Are you all right? Can I do something?"

"Yes, Erik," she replied. "I want you to help Rolf. He is going to this new area to find his brother and a place for us to live. I need you to help him."

Erik swallowed hard. "What about you and Elsa?"

"We'll be fine here," she said. "Mrs. Haugen is kind. I'm not sick, just tired. I'll feel better soon. Then we can join you."

"This house is small," Erik said.

"There's another room. They're storing merchandise in it, but Mr. Haugen said he will make space for Elsa and me. It will only be for a few weeks."

Weeks. Erik had been thinking days. He nodded his head. "Yes, Ma," he said.

Going back outside, Erik saw Mr. Haugen on the borrowed wagon.

"Come for a ride, Erik?"

"I don't think I have time," Erik began, but Mr. Haugen interrupted.

"We won't be long," he said. "Your father has gone to get some supplies. We'll be back before he is."

"Supplies?" repeated Erik. How many supplies did they need? They already had more than the wagon could hold.

"Food," said Mr. Haugen, as Erik jumped up beside him. "You need to eat. I think he said something about a fishing rod, too."

Erik's head jerked up at that. A fishing rod? Where would they fish? Then he remembered the river valley that was to give the new town its name.

"Have you ever driven horses?" Mr. Haugen asked.

"*Ja!* On my grandfather's farm."

"Then why don't you drive? We're just going to the edge of town."

Erik took the reins eagerly, feeling the strength of the big black horses through the leather. Why had Rolf bought Black and Socks when he could have had beautiful horses like these?

When they reached the paddock by a small white house, they unhitched the horses and turned them loose. They were bigger than Erik's grandfather's horses, bigger than what he'd want for a riding horse, but they were so much better than oxen. They had personality. Oxen were just stupid cows!

"Perhaps Rolf will buy a team like this after you get your first crop," suggested Mr. Haugen.

Erik nodded. "Perhaps," he agreed politely, but he couldn't imagine it happening, not with Rolf doing the farming. All Rolf knew was how to cut down trees.

They walked quickly back to the lumberyard. Mr. Haugen went in the front door of the store. Erik perched on some fenceposts in the shade of a pile of lumber to wait for Rolf.

Two men in wide-brimmed hats came down the boardwalk toward him, a young man with a wispy brown beard and an older man with bushy eyebrows and a dark moustache drooping past his chin. They were the same men who'd bumped into Erik on the street the day before.

"Has Pete made any plans yet?" the younger man asked in English. Erik listened carefully, translating the words in his head.

The older man grunted. "You know Pete. He always has plans. Good ones, too."

Erik was pleased that he could understand the gist of the men's conversation. Those three months of school in Minnesota had been good for his English.

"They're not all good, Tex. Remember Colorado?"

"We're not in jail, are we?" Tex thumped the other man on the back. "We're safe here, Jim. In a place like this, no one's gonna ask questions and no one's gonna care."

Erik stared at their retreating backs. He must have misunderstood. Maybe *jail* had another English meaning that he hadn't learned.

"Did you yoke the oxen?" asked Rolf. Erik jumped. He had been so intent on the cowboys he hadn't noticed Rolf behind them carrying a large paper-wrapped parcel.

He pulled out the oxen's tether stakes while Rolf secured the parcel under the canvas in the wagon. They yoked the oxen, then Erik tied the cow on behind and Rolf swung the chicken cage onto the wagon.

Still without speaking, Rolf went into the house. Erik watched him go.

Erik had sympathized with Elsa staying with Mrs. Hanson, but he wondered if working alone with Rolf wasn't going to be worse.

CHAPTER THREE

Travelling

The trail out of Hanley was well worn, with home-steads every kilometre or so. Erik noted each one, wondering what theirs would be like. Sometimes he couldn't see a house, just two or three low sheds. All the farms looked poor compared to his grandfather's, with its fine barn and strong fences.

Erik glanced sideways at Rolf. He was rolling the whip between his hands restlessly. There were no reins to hold and the whip was rarely needed. The oxen were trained to respond to voice signals. English voice signals.

The homestead coming up was another one of those where Erik couldn't see a house. He knew there had to be one. Clothes hung on a line and children played nearby.

Smoke rose from a chimney pipe on one of the low buildings. A woman stepped through the door. She waved her arm in greeting, then strode across the yard, a metal pail in one hand.

Erik could hardly believe what he was seeing.

"That house is made of dirt!" he exclaimed. "There's grass growing on the roof!"

"A sod house," said Rolf, nodding. He laid the whip across his legs and took off his hat, running his hands through his red hair till it stood on end. "We'll probably build one of those." He shoved the hat back on his head.

"A dirt house!" said Erik, horrified. "Ma doesn't want to live in a dirt house."

"Your mother knows that things are different here. You need to know that, too."

Erik bit the inside of his lip, choking back an angry reply.

Dirt houses, slow oxen, no trees. What kind of a land had they come to?

He watched the oxen for a moment. He could walk as fast as they could. Or faster. Without a word, he stood up and jumped off the wagon, landing in the dusty grass by the trail.

Behind the wagon, Erik glared at Rolf. He'd never known anyone so hard to talk to.

Rolf called out to the oxen, tapping Black lightly on a shoulder to steer around water lying on the trail. Erik admitted to himself that Rolf seemed to know how to handle the oxen all right. He'd bought them from the farmer he'd worked for during their three months in Minnesota, so they were used to each other.

The farmer had told Rolf that oxen were stronger than horses for breaking sod and could work on poorer feed. From what Erik could see, Saskatchewan had lots of both. Sod and poor feed.

The whole country looked flat – flat like a plate. He missed the mountains, the green. It was green here, but a duller green. The homesteads were dull, too, with few painted buildings.

It had been cool when they left Hanley, but it grew hotter each hour. Tired and sweaty, Erik swung back onto the moving wagon. Moments later Rolf handed him the whip and jumped down.

The sun was high overhead and Erik's stomach was grumbling by the time they reached a shallow creek. The oxen refused to enter the water till Rolf walked beside them. The water splashed the wagon and the oxen moved even more slowly, searching for traction beneath their feet. Erik felt useless, sitting on the wagon. Rolf had the whip so he couldn't even pretend he was helping. Once on dry land, Rolf, his trousers dripping, put his boots back on. Erik dug out the meal Mrs. Haugen had packed in a red lard pail. While the cattle grazed, they ate the soft white bread, slices of cooked beef and rhubarb turnovers.

There were more of the little pies in the wagon, Erik knew. He pictured them in his mind, counting how many there were and how many meals they would have before they arrived at Lars's place. He hoped his mother learned how to make them while she stayed with the Haugens.

When they finished eating, Rolf stretched out on the ground, his cap covering his face. Erik led Tess and the oxen to the creek to drink, then brought water to the chickens. The moment he was done, Rolf stood up.

Erik rode for the first stretch while the June sun beat down on his head, hotter than anything he remembered in Norway.

As the afternoon progressed they saw fewer home-steads and more undisturbed prairie. To keep himself from falling asleep, Erik jumped down and walked again. The day seemed as long as three days.

A small brown animal popped out of a hole on his left and ran down the trail toward him. It stopped suddenly and sat up on its hind legs, looking around.

It made Erik think of a squirrel with most of its tail missing.

He took a step toward the animal. It whistled sharply, then dropped back on four feet and ran into the grass. Stopping beside a small mound of dirt, it whistled again, then disappeared into the ground. Erik ran toward the hole, but when he got there, the animal was gone.

Looking up, he couldn't see the wagon.

Erik ran along the trail, feeling the upward slope as he ran, surprised to discover the land wasn't as flat as it looked. He hoped Rolf hadn't noticed how far behind he was. As he crested the slight hill, he saw the wagon. The breeze cooled his face as he ran, lifting his hat and tossing it into the grass.

At sundown, Rolf stopped the wagon by a pond, frightening ducks into the reeds. Green-headed ducks, just like the ones at home in Norway.

Erik thought about roasted duck as he filled the coffee pot with water. He'd never shot a gun, but in this new country he hoped to learn.

Later, rolled into a quilt, Erik gazed sleepily at the stars until a cloud of whining insects surrounded him, stinging his face. He slapped them away, then pulled the blanket over his head. It was stuffy and hot under the scratchy blanket, but at least he wasn't being bitten.

It was still dark when Rolf's hand, heavy on Erik's shoulder, shook him awake.

"Get under the wagon," Rolf ordered, a flash of lightning illuminating his bearded face. "I'm going to check the cover." Startled, Erik realized his hair, sticking out from under the blanket, was damp. Wind tore at his bedding and whipped the canvas on the wagon.

Thunder rolled.

Erik jumped to his feet and grabbed his quilts. Slithering under the wagon, he spread them out. Finding Rolf's bedding behind a wheel, he spread it too. Rolf joined Erik under the wagon a minute later.

"*Takk,*" he said gruffly.

A streak of lightning revealed the wooden crate near the pond.

"The chickens!" exclaimed Erik. "We need to bring them under the wagon, too."

"I'm not sleeping with chickens," said Rolf. "They'll be fine."

"The cattle will be fine," said Erik. "The chickens need to be out of the rain."

Rolf didn't reply.

Good, thought Erik. If Rolf didn't care, why should he? Rolf was in charge.

But Erik's mother always put the chickens in the henhouse when it rained.

Another flash of lightning was followed almost immediately by a deafening clap of thunder. The rain pelted down harder.

Erik pushed his blanket back and crawled out from under the wagon.

Wind drove the rain against him, drenching his hair, soaking through his shirt. Norway had thunderstorms, but Erik had never seen any this wild.

A bolt of lightning sliced the sky. He ran toward the crate, sliding on the rain-slicked ground. The wagon seemed further away on the return trip, and Erik prayed for lightning to guide his way.

He received more than he wanted, with bolts of lightning on every side and an almost simultaneous crack of thunder that seemed to go on forever.

Hurriedly Erik slipped the crate of drenched birds under the end of the wagon closest to Rolf's feet. A moment later he slid underneath himself. Cold and wet, he wrapped himself in his quilt.

The lightning was so close. What if it hit one of the oxen? Or the wagon?

At least he didn't need to worry about the wet chickens bothering Rolf. In a break between claps of thunder, Erik heard him snore.

How could Rolf sleep through the noise?

Erik closed his eyes. And opened them again.

Shivering, he listened to the storm. Watched the lightning flash. Were his dreams of being a farmer going to end now, underneath the wagon?

He'd always wanted to farm, helping with the goats since he was small, with field work as he grew older. His grandfather said Erik would make a fine farmer. But Grandfather's farm would be Uncle Svend's one day.

Around them were mountains and more farmers with more sons. Norway didn't have enough land for all the men who wanted to farm.

After Svend married, Inga told Erik and Elsa that she was marrying Rolf. "He's a good man," she'd said. "He'll give us a home in the village and take care of us."

But he hadn't. He'd brought them here. To be wet and cold under a wagon while a storm raged all around.

The wind blew rain under the wagon, soaking through the blankets, his jacket, his shirt. Erik couldn't remember when he'd been so cold, or felt so lonely.

Morning was cloudy and much cooler than the day before. Erik spread his bedding over the canvas on the wagon and hoped it would dry as they travelled.

Rolf struggled to light a fire, finally boiling some coffee. Erik led the cattle to the pond, then pulled the crate of chickens from under the wagon. Their feathers clung to their skinny bodies, but they pecked eagerly at the grain he gave them.

Rolf handed Erik his coffee. "I see the rain ran under your side of the wagon."

Erik wrapped his hands around the warm tin cup.

"Could be," he replied, wondering if Rolf had noticed he'd moved the chickens.

"You'll dry once we get going." Rolf cocked an eye at the clouds. "I expect it'll clear up soon."

"*Ja,*" said Erik, wishing that Rolf would offer him dry clothes, knowing it was too much trouble to find them in

23

the tightly packed wagon.

Rolf steered the oxen away from the muddy trail and onto the grass where the pulling was a little easier.

Erik walked behind, cold in the wind. After a while he climbed up beside Rolf. He was tired of walking, tired of the oxen, tired of travelling.

He'd hated the ocean voyage. He'd thought the ship too small to cross anything as wide as the Atlantic Ocean. He and his mother had been seasick most of the way, leaving Elsa and Rolf to explore the ship and watch the sea.

Erik's father had been a fisherman, making his living on the ocean. When Erik was three, his father died in a storm at sea. Every day of their crossing, Erik had prayed that it wouldn't storm, that the ship would make it safely to America.

If he hadn't wanted to be a farmer, he would have fought against leaving Norway. He would have fought against getting on that ship. He'd only come because he knew that in America he could be a farmer.

In the afternoon they met a wagon pulled by a team of four horses. Rolf stopped the oxen.

The approaching wagon stopped as well. Erik thought the red-haired driver looked only a few years older than him. The young man looked from Rolf to Erik and back to Rolf.

"Good day," said Rolf in English. "We seek Lars Hanson."

The young man didn't answer right away, staring at Rolf, his eyes cold. Though Rolf had spoken English, he answered in Norwegian. "Two miles ahead and one mile west. You'll know it by the piles of lumber." He slapped the reins against the horses and started moving.

"*Takk,*" said Rolf. "Thank you." But the empty wagon had already rattled past.

"How did he know we understood Norwegian?" Erik said, surprised.

Rolf twisted on the seat, watching the retreating wagon.

After a long moment, he shook his head slightly. "I don't know," he said. "I don't know."

He called out to the oxen and they plodded forward.

Erik felt almost lightheaded with relief, knowing their long journey was nearly over.

Rolf, on the other hand, didn't seem happy at all. Glancing at his hand holding the whip, Erik saw it was shaking.

CHAPTER FOUR

Lefsa

A man stacking lumber turned as they drove into the yard. Big, broad-shouldered and red-bearded, he could have been Rolf's twin. As the wagon drew closer, his face split into a grin.

"It's about time, little brother."

Rolf was barely down from the wagon when his brother had his hands on his arms, pulling him into a hug.

"Lars," said Rolf, his voice sounding weak. "You are here."

"Of course I'm here." Lars laughed, a deep booming sound, and hugged Rolf again. "What is amazing is that you are here. I hoped you would come, but when you didn't answer my letter and then we moved –"

"And moved again," interrupted Rolf.

"*Ja, ja,* you are right," said Lars, still laughing. "I moved again, but always I left a trail for you to follow, did I not? And look, you're here." He suddenly sobered. "But you've missed Olaf. He left a short while ago to get another load of lumber from Hanley."

Rolf went still.

Lars stepped back, his smile suddenly looked forced.

"But Kirsten is inside. Come in, come in. She'll be glad to see you." His eyes settled on Erik. "And who is this young man, and why haven't you introduced us?"

Rolf swung around, seeming surprised to see Erik standing by the wagon.

"Erik," he said stiffly. "This is Erik Brekke."

"Erik!" exclaimed Lars, coming around the oxen toward him, arms outstretched. Erik stepped back instinctively, but instead of hugging him, Lars took one hand in both of his, pumping it up and down. "Come in, come in. We'll have coffee and *lefsa* and you can tell me how you come to be with this brother of mine. With that name, you must be from the homeland, too?"

At Erik's nod, he smiled broadly. "Welcome, welcome!"

Lars turned back to Rolf and half-led, half-pushed him toward the house, his arm across Rolf's back.

"The cattle –" Rolf began.

"They will wait till you greet Kirsten and have some coffee," Lars said firmly. "The pot is on."

Erik saw a water trough off to one side. He started to unfasten the yoke.

"No, no, boy. Coffee for you, too. The oxen will wait."

Erik hesitated. His grandfather had taught him to care for the livestock first. "They can't do it themselves," he'd explained to Erik. "So you have to do it for them."

"It won't take long," Erik said.

"Can we tether them on the grass?" Rolf asked.

Lars waved his arm in a wide circle. "Certainly," he said. "There is grass all around."

A few minutes later, Erik joined the others in the house, a single room with a bed in one corner. Mr. Haugen had said the building would become a store after they moved it to Green Valley. Erik could see it was built in the same style as the stores they'd seen in Hanley.

Lars and Rolf drank coffee at a small wooden table by the large front window. A woman flipped a circle of dough at the stove. She turned to Erik with a smile as Lars introduced them.

"Hello, Erik," she said warmly. *"Velkommen."*

Erik greeted her, looking hungrily at the stack of fresh potato flatbreads on the table.

Kirsten placed a thin brown-flecked circle on a plate and handed it to Erik.

Lars indicated a stool and poured Erik a cup of strong black coffee.

Erik spread the *lefsa* with soft butter that melted on contact, sprinkled it with sugar, then folded it into quarters. Firmer than Mrs. Haugen's white bread, softer than his mother's dry flatbread, the *lefsa* tasted faintly of the potatoes used to make it.

"So you'll be looking for land, now, will you, Rolf?" Lars asked as he settled back into his own chair. "It's a pity there's so little homesteading land left right around here."

"So little?" asked Rolf. "We saw uncultivated land most of the way from Hanley." He set down his coffee cup and accepted a warm *lefsa* from Kirsten.

"Most of it belongs to the railroads," said Lars. "It's still a good price, but not free like the homestead land. The only homestead quarters available within miles are hilly pieces close to the river, and no good for crops." He turned to Erik, "But you, Erik, you're too young to buy a farm."

Erik swallowed quickly. "I helped my grandfather," he said. He took another bite of *lefsa* so he wouldn't have to talk.

"He will help me," Rolf said. "We must find land and a place to live so we can bring Inga and Elsa here."

"Inga?" repeated Lars. "Elsa?"

"My wife, Inga," said Rolf. "I wrote to you about her. Didn't you get my letter?

"I've had no letter since you wrote to say that *Mor* had passed on." Lars turned to Kirsten. "Did you hear that, Kirsten? Rolf has a wife after all these years."

"I'm happy for you, Rolf," she said, plopping a fresh *lefsa* down in front of Erik.

"I'm guessing that you are Inga's son," she said with a smile. Erik nodded, but Rolf answered before he could.

"Yes, she has two children, Erik and Elsa. Elsa and Inga are in Hanley with Gunnar and Luise Haugen. Erik and I need to find a home, then we will bring them to join us."

"This is excellent," exclaimed Lars. "I'm so happy to have a new sister, and a nephew and niece," he added, smiling at Erik. He reached for the coffee pot. "One more cup, then we look for land."

Erik and Rolf spent the next few days with Lars in his buggy. Leaving the oxen tethered by the piles of lumber, Rolf and Lars talked and Erik listened as they met people, looked at land and learned about sod houses. One of the settlers, Mr. Johnson, told them how to build the house, even lending the plough needed for cutting the sod.

To Erik, everywhere looked the same. It was a land without landmarks. Each night they returned to sleep in the canvas tent. Once they saw lumber had been added to the piles, but again they'd missed Olaf.

After much thought, Rolf arranged to buy a quarter section from the railway company. It cost $2.50 an acre, much more than the ten dollars required for homestead land. He paid seventy dollars immediately, with the remaining three hundred and thirty dollars spread over the next five years.

Erik watched Rolf count out the bills, surprised Rolf still had seventy dollars left after paying for their trip from Norway and all the supplies.

Now they had to get a crop or they'd lose it all.

When Rolf and Erik drove to the land on their own, they stopped a couple of times to check the survey markers.

"This is it," said Rolf, looking at one of the markers. "My land." He stretched his arms wide. *"Our land."*

Erik eyed the expanse of short grass, trying to imagine a home, a barn, corrals…built from what? All they had was the land on which they stood and a wagon full of furniture and supplies.

Not far away, he saw what looked to be short, weedy plants growing among the grass. As they drew closer, he realized they were short bushes growing around water that had pooled in a dip in the land.

"It's a slough," said Rolf. "Lars says that's what they call ponds here. It dries up when there's no rain, and fills with water in the spring."

Erik tried to imagine the slough full of water. If there was more water, wouldn't the plants and bushes drown?

"We must choose a spot for our house. Close to the slough, for water," Rolf suggested, "but not too close, or we may have too much water sometimes."

Erik nodded. In the shelter of trees would be good, he thought, if only there were trees.

Rolf started to untie the canvas covering the wagon. "What do you think?" he asked abruptly.

"Think?" Erik repeated, surprised. "I – I don't know."

Rolf pulled a spade from under the canvas. "Where's the sun going to rise in the morning?"

Erik pointed east and Rolf nodded. He turned slowly in a circle.

"A hill would be better," said Rolf. "When you build against a hill, you only need to build three walls."

Rolf walked a short distance, turned, walked again. Finally he stopped about thirty metres from the slough and drove the spade into the ground.

"This is where our house will be," he said. "But if it is a bad choice, it doesn't matter. We will build a new house soon. A house from wood, next time."

Erik nodded. He hoped his mother wouldn't be too

sad to move into a sod house. Erik wasn't happy about it, himself. The ones they'd visited were dark, with low ceilings. Some had wooden floors, but most were packed dirt.

"It's good we're not the first," Erik said suddenly.

"The first?" repeated Rolf.

"Ja," said Erik. "The first to settle here. This way we learn from others, and we can eat Aunt Kirsten's cooking."

Rolf smiled. "You're right, Erik. It's good we're not the first."

Erik couldn't help smiling back. He and Rolf had agreed on something!

Rolf moved the wagon closer to where they would build, then tethered the oxen by the slough. Erik tethered the cow nearby and lifted down the chickens.

"We can't tether these," said Erik.

"I don't know anything about chickens," said Rolf. "You decide what to do with them."

Erik carried the crate awkwardly down to the slough, setting it out of the wind beside some of the shrubby bushes. He brought grain and water, watching them doubtfully. One of the hens pecked at leaves through the mesh of the chicken wire. There were just five birds in the cage, four hens and a rooster.

"Maybe tomorrow," he said at last. "I'll let you out tomorrow."

Rolf used his spade to mark out the walls of the sod house. He planned for two rooms, the smaller with bunks for Elsa and Erik. The main room would serve as kitchen and sitting room as well as a place for Rolf and Inga to sleep.

"We might as well get started," said Rolf, looking at the marks he'd made in the dirt.

Erik nodded. He didn't want a sod house, but it was better than no house at all. He helped Rolf hitch the oxen to the borrowed plough, then watched as he cut strips of sod from the rectangle that would be the house. When he was finished there, Rolf paced off the perimeter of the yard. He and the oxen began cutting sods from around it to make a firebreak while Erik started to build the house.

He cut each strip of sod into metre-long lengths, then laid the heavy, awkward blocks in a double row to start the walls. He overlapped the second row like bricks. The roots of the grass held most of the soil in place, but small pieces fell out as Erik carried them.

They stopped at noon to set up the tent. Rolf unloaded what they needed from the wagon while Erik boiled water from the slough for coffee. When they finally sat down to flatbread and *gjetost,* Erik was so hungry that he forgot he was sick of the goat cheese.

After lunch, Erik laid the sods for the third layer at right angles to the first two rows. Mr. Johnson had said that was the key to strong walls.

The work got suddenly harder when Erik laid the last sod cut from the floor of the house and began carrying them from the firebreak. A metre long by half a metre wide and ten centimetres thick. Who knew dirt was so heavy?

CHAPTER FIVE

Cousins?

The next morning Erik woke to birdsong. The sun was already hot on the walls of the tent, filling it with the odour of warm canvas. He stretched cautiously, his arms and back aching from carrying sod.

The rooster crowed and one of the oxen bellowed. Rolf was still asleep.

The rooster crowed again as Erik crawled out of the tent.

"*Ja, Ja!*" said Erik. "I'll let you out." As soon as he opened the crate door, the chickens crowded through the opening.

He jumped out of reach of a hen trying to peck his bare toes, then checked the cattle. Black was eating the short grass by the slough. Socks lay nearby, chewing his cud, but Tess's rope lay useless on the ground, the end frayed and broken.

Forgetting his tired muscles, Erik ran and pulled the tether stake out of the ground. He wrapped the rope around his arm and looked around. He should be able to see the cow, since there was nothing to block the view. Shading his eyes against the morning sun, he saw something move far off in the east. He started running, keeping his eyes on the brown shape in the distance.

Yes, it was definitely a cow. A little closer and he saw Tess was not alone. At her side was a brown-and-white calf.

Erik stood still, watching Tess lick the calf's head. The calf wobbled a bit and fell down. Tess nudged it with her nose. It scrambled back to its feet, hind end first, while Tess licked along its back.

It was a miracle. They'd bought one animal and now there were two.

Erik grinned as the gangly legged calf head-butted its mother in the side, then, tail wagging, started to suck.

Erik's stomach growled, urging him to get back for breakfast. Moving slowly, he circled around till the cow and calf were between him and the yard site. He put one cautious foot forward, then the other.

Tess took a couple of steps away from Erik. The calf bleated in protest.

Erik moved closer to the cow. Tess kept walking, but the calf didn't move.

A sudden pain knifed through Erik's foot. He yelped in surprise, hopping on one leg. The calf turned at the sound, saw Erik, and ran to its mother.

Drops of blood dripped from the Erik's bare foot. Looking at the ground, he saw a plant with a yellow flower and pointed spines all over its fat green leaves. Touching a spine carefully with the tip of a finger, he found it sharp as a needle.

Erik rubbed the sole of his foot for a moment, then gingerly set it down. Tess was licking her calf again. Speaking softly, he limped over to the cow, slipped the rope around her neck, and tied it quickly. The calf dropped to the ground, closing its eyes.

"You can't stop now!" Erik nudged the calf with his foot. "If you stay out here, a wolf will get you."

Getting no response from the calf, he grabbed it with his free arm and pulled it to its feet. The calf bleated in protest and flopped back on the ground.

Erik pulled it up again. It took a few steps, then stopped. Erik let it suck for another moment, then gave Tess's rope a tug.

By the time they straggled back to the yard, Rolf had eaten breakfast and hitched the oxen to the plough. He watched Erik lead Tess to the slough.

"You and the cow went for a walk?" he asked.

"*Ja,*" Erik replied. "But Tess went first."

"Good you came home together." Rolf scratched the calf's head. "Fine heifer calf."

"It's a tired calf," said Erik, hammering the cow's tether stake into the ground.

"We haven't built a barn or ploughed a field," said Rolf, "but our farm is already growing."

Erik looked from Rolf to the calf and back again. "It's a start," he said.

He poured himself a cup of coffee and grabbed a chunk of the hard, dry flatbread his mother had made in Minnesota. Still chewing, he grabbed the knife and went to cut the sods as Rolf ploughed. His foot still stung from the spiny plant, but it was nothing compared to the ache in his arms from carrying the sods.

Early in the evening, Rolf tethered the oxen. Erik laid

the last of the prepared sods while Rolf unloaded the wagon. "Tomorrow," he said, "we'll see Lars for wood to make window and door frames."

Erik looked at the house. The walls were above his knees, but he thought them too low for the amount of work they'd done.

The next morning, a wagon rattled into the yard as they finished breakfast. Lars sat on the wooden seat beside the red-headed young man Erik and Rolf had met on the trail when they first arrived in the district.

He must be Olaf, Erik realized. His cousin, or step-cousin if there was such a thing.

"We've come to help," said Lars, pulling the horses to a stop. "Unless you're done?" He grinned at Erik.

"Olaf," said Rolf, ignoring his brother. His voice was high-pitched and unlike himself. "I didn't know it was you the other day, when we met."

Olaf looked at Rolf. He opened his mouth but no words came out.

"Olaf," said Lars. "This is Erik Brekke, the son of Rolf's new wife, Inga."

"Good morning," said Erik.

Olaf shot him a quick glance and an even quicker nod.

Lars turned to Rolf. "I found a few pieces of lumber lying around. Perhaps you can use them in your house."

"*Manga takk,* Lars," said Rolf, still looking at Olaf. "We were just going to visit you to buy wood to make a door."

Lars climbed down from the wagon and gestured to Erik. "Help me unload this," he said. "We'll leave those

37

two to stare at each other."

As Lars spoke, Olaf deliberately looked away from Rolf and climbed down on the other side of the wagon.

Confused, Erik helped Lars lay the boards in a pile.

"Olaf," Rolf said, still in that strange voice. "It's been so many years. You've grown to be a man." He moved around the wagon, his hand outstretched.

Olaf looked at the hand. *"Ja,"* he said, his voice hard. "Many years." Turning his back on Rolf, he tugged on one of the boards in the wagon.

Rolf stood a moment longer, his hand still out in front of him.

"You help Olaf with that long one," Lars told Erik. "Rolf can show me what he has planned."

He went over to Rolf and laid his hand on his shoulder. "Show me your house, Rolf," he said. "You've made progress in a short time."

Rolf seemed to give himself a shake. "Certainly," he said. "Erik is a hard worker."

Erik almost dropped the piece of wood he'd just picked up. Rolf had said something nice about him! He took a firmer hold on the wood, trying not to show how pleased he felt. At the other end of the plank, Olaf scowled.

While the brothers made window and door frames, Olaf joined Erik laying sods. They worked silently. Olaf's sullen face didn't invite conversation.

When the framing was done, Lars fastened together strips of wood to make a door, while Rolf went back to ploughing.

Using Lars's team, Olaf and Erik stacked the sods in

the wagon instead of carrying them one by one to the house. Olaf worked swiftly, effortlessly lifting each heavy sod into place. Erik pushed himself to keep up, but Olaf moved two sods for each one of Erik's.

When they stopped at noon to eat tinned beans, Lars admired the rising walls.

"Perhaps you should start filling in the cracks," he said to Erik. "Olaf can keep laying sod. What do you think, Olaf?"

Erik looked up from his plate. Filling cracks sounded easier than hauling sods, but he didn't want them to think he couldn't do the hard work.

"It doesn't matter," said Olaf indifferently. "It all needs to be done."

"What do we fill the cracks with?" asked Erik, trying to remember what Mr. Johnson had told them.

"Mud from the slough," said Lars. He glanced at his son. "Olaf can show you how to do it."

"I can figure it out," said Erik. He didn't want to ask Olaf anything.

"Good," said Lars, handing mugs of coffee to his silent brother and son. "Isn't it great working together?"

No one replied, but Lars didn't seem to mind. He took a sip of his coffee and glanced at Rolf. "The slough water's not bad now," he said, "but later on you'll want to get water from the spring."

"A spring?" repeated Erik. "There's a spring around here?"

"Surely is," said Lars. "Couple of miles northwest. I'll draw you a map so you can find it."

After they ate, Rolf and Lars stretched out on the grass and closed their eyes, appearing to fall asleep immediately. Erik looked at them, surprised that brothers, separated for so many years, could still be so similar.

He gathered a metal pail and spade and headed for the slough. The cattle lay in a contented group; the chickens scratched in the dirt nearby. The calf bounced up as Erik approached, running to hide behind its mother. Erik held out a hand, talking softly, but the calf watched him warily, not moving.

"Next time," he said, dropping his hand. He filled the pail with mud, then lugged it back to the sod house.

Olaf was at work already, lifting a sod from the wagon. He turned to glance at Erik. "Pack it tight," he said. "So the snakes can't get in."

Snakes? How could they keep snakes out? They lived in dirt.

Erik sighed and forced the first handful of mud into the cracks between the layers of sods, determined to keep anything from creeping through.

As he reached for another handful, he saw Olaf still watching him.

He looked less angry, so Erik risked a question. "Have you built a sod house before?" he asked.

"*Ja,*" said Olaf. He swung the sod onto the wall. "I've worked at many things. I build with Gunnar Haugen and my –" he stopped speaking as he positioned the sod perfectly, then started again. "I've built with wood and I've built with sod. Sometimes I dig holes for people, or I drive wagons. I do any work I can to earn money."

Erik looked at him with respect. "What do you do with your money?" he asked. "Do you give it to Uncle Lars?"

"No. He says, 'Keep the money, Olaf, and buy yourself some land.'" Olaf reached for another sod and glanced over his shoulder at Erik. "So I put the money in the bank in Hanley, and one day I'll buy myself some land."

"When?"

"When I'm eighteen, or maybe seventeen." Erik looked at him, wondering how old he was now. "I'll be sixteen soon," said Olaf, answering Erik's look.

"In September," said Rolf.

Erik looked up in surprise. He hadn't seen him coming.

"September 9th," Rolf added. "I'll never forget that day."

Olaf carried the sod to the wall without looking at Rolf. Rolf watched him lay the sod in place, then turned away, his shoulders sagging.

Two days later Olaf laid the last sods on the walls of the house. He made the front wall of the house two layers taller than the back wall, then sloped the sides toward the back.

Erik dug handfuls of mud from his pail, trying to smooth the inside walls, keeping one eye on Lars and Rolf laying poles above his head. When Rolf spread tarpaper across the poles, the house grew dim.

Erik refilled his pail with mud. On the way back from the slough, he saw the men were laying the sods on the roof with the grass side up.

Inside the house, dust sifted through where the sheets of tarpaper overlapped. Rolf poked his head in the door and glanced around. "It won't be so dusty when the sods settle," he said.

"What will happen when it rains?" asked Erik, but Rolf was already gone.

When the roof was covered with sod, they carried the furniture in from the wagon, piling it in the centre of the room. Erik chased a chicken out of the house, then stood in the doorway to keep it from coming back.

Even with the windows, it seemed dark in the house. Dark as a barn, dark as a cave.

"We'll buy wood to divide the rooms," Rolf added. "Later."

"You should whitewash the walls," Lars said. "It will be brighter for your Inga."

"*Ja,*" said Rolf, but it was Erik who ended up brushing the mixture of lime, salt, and water on the walls. Olaf rode up on a horse the next morning while they were mixing the whitewash.

"Your brother thinks you need more help," he said, not looking at Rolf.

"Don't you have more lumber to bring from Hanley?" Rolf asked stiffly.

Olaf shrugged. "He says it will wait." He glanced around, gesturing to a few poles left from making the roof. "What are you doing with those?"

Rolf glanced at the pile. "I'll need most of them for the outhouse," he said.

"If there's extra," suggested Olaf, "you could start a

corral."

"Do we need one?" asked Rolf. "The cattle seem content being tethered."

Olaf shrugged his shoulders. His expression said he didn't care. It wasn't *his* farm.

"It might be good," said Erik, "especially for the calf." Right now the calf never strayed far from its mother, but it would grow more adventurous.

Erik listened to Olaf and Rolf rummage through the small pile of poles while he stirred the thin whitewash mixture. He wondered why Rolf and Olaf had so much trouble speaking to each other. It was even worse than him and Rolf.

After a few minutes, Rolf dragged a few of the poles behind the house, while Olaf began cutting the others in half.

Erik dipped his brush into the pail and ran it down the wall. When he dipped a second time, specks of dirt floated in the whitewash. After he painted a section, he stepped back and looked. He could tell where he'd brushed, but he couldn't call it white.

While he worked, Erik thought of life in Norway. He'd never worked this hard there. He'd helped Grandfather in the mornings before breakfast, and sometimes he'd go out again before supper, but he and Elsa were both at school much of the day.

No one had mentioned school since they'd left Minnesota.

They stopped briefly at noon to eat soup Kirsten had sent with Olaf, then went right back to work. An

ADELE DUECK

hour or so later, Erik stopped for a rest, laying his brush across the pail.

Hearing a raised voice, he looked out the open doorway. Olaf stood by a corral post, glaring at Rolf a couple of metres away.

"I've been helping all week," said Olaf, "and you haven't said a word."

"What do you mean? I talk to you every day."

"Right," said Olaf. "About work I should do and if the wind will stop blowing. Not one word about how you didn't want me. Gave me away. Never wrote in all the years we were here."

"I wrote to Lars," Rolf protested. "I didn't know what to say to you. You were just five years old."

"*Ja!* Five years old! I come and work for you every day. *For free!* And you talk about me being five years old!"

"That's not what I meant," exclaimed Rolf, his voice rising. "You are a man now, I see that. I don't know –"

"That's for certain you don't know," said Olaf angrily. "You don't know how to be a father and I doubt you know how to be a farmer, either. What farming have you ever done?"

"I will learn," Rolf began, but Olaf threw his spade to the ground and strode angrily toward his horse.

"I'm going back to my *real* parents," he said over his shoulder. "You can build your own farm. You and your *new* son."

Rolf yelled something to Olaf, but Erik could barely hear it over the sound of the horse's hooves. It sounded like "I came here to find you."

CHAPTER SIX

Discovery

Erik stepped backwards into the house. Grabbing the paintbrush, he finished the first coat of whitewash and started the second. While his hands worked, Olaf's words echoed in his head. "You and your *new* son." It could mean only one thing.

Rolf was Olaf's father.

They were father and son, but they hadn't seen each other in ten years.

Erik stood still, the brush suspended in the air. He hadn't seen *his* father in nine years. It was bad enough having a father who died. Wouldn't it be worse if his father had given him away?

And Olaf thought Erik was taking his place. What a joke! Erik didn't consider Rolf his father, and Rolf certainly didn't see Erik as his son.

Had he heard Rolf correctly? Had he come to America just to see his son again? But if that was his only goal, he had no reason to get married, no reason to bring a family with him.

Erik watched whitewash drip from his brush onto the dirt floor. Shaking his head, he dipped the brush in the pail. What did it matter, anyway? He, Erik, had come to be a farmer. Olaf didn't make any difference to his plans. And Ma? Erik thought for a moment. It wasn't going to matter to her either, because he was certain she knew about Olaf already.

Later, his pail empty, Erik cautiously poked his head out the door. There was no sign of Rolf. He peered into the hole Rolf had been digging.

"How's the whitewashing?"

The sudden voice behind him made Erik jump and spin around.

"I need to mix up some more."

"Then you better do it," said Rolf, lowering himself into the hole.

"I'm about to," said Erik stiffly. Did Rolf think he wasn't going to finish the work? "I was just seeing if you needed anything."

"What should I need?" asked Rolf, raising the pick high and driving it into the hard grey subsoil.

Instead of answering, Erik swung around and headed for the house, hot anger burning in his throat.

He avoided talking to Rolf for the rest of the day. It wasn't hard, because Rolf didn't talk to him either. The next day Rolf acted as if nothing had happened. He even smiled when he saw the finished walls. "Good work," he said.

They moved the furniture into place and assembled the pipes for the small, round stove.

"I guess we can sleep in here now," said Rolf.

Erik looked at the bed they'd put together for Rolf

and Inga. There was no bed for him or Elsa. "I'll stay in the tent," he said. "At least for now."

"If you like," said Rolf.

Erik moved to the doorway, anxious to get out of the dim house, so different from their home in Norway.

"When are we going to get *Mor* and Elsa?"

"I need to finish the outhouse," Rolf said.

"They would want to be here."

"*Ja*. You're right about that."

Rolf passed Erik, going out into the sunshine.

"Soon," he said. "Later this week."

Erik wondered what day it was, how many days were left in the week. Since they'd left Hanley, every day had felt the same.

Rolf picked up the canvas that had covered the wagon and dragged it over to the hole. He dropped it to the ground nearby, then went back for the few pieces of wood left by the house. He looked at the pile, nudging the pieces with his foot.

Erik watched him silently. Finally Rolf looked up. "Why don't we see what's in that river?" he said. "Maybe catch us a fish for supper?"

They walked straight west from the sod house. Erik carried the fishing poles Rolf had bought in Hanley; Rolf had flatbread and tin cups in a pail.

The prairie was as flat as the land around their sod house. The grass grew thin and dusty green.

Erik kicked at a clump of grass. Unexpectedly, a flash of purple caught his eye. Looking closer he saw miniature flowers mingled with the grass. Further on he found scattered bones, bleached white, half buried in the sod.

Buffalo bones! Hoping for more, Erik was startled by a pale brown bird flying out of the grass right in front of him.

After crossing several quarters of land, Erik noticed the land changing. It fell and rose, then seemed to come to an end, just ahead, where Rolf stood without moving.

Erik stopped beside him.

Below lay the river – wide and swift and clear, the banks on both sides green with bushes. Erik hadn't seen any sign of the trees Mr. Haugen had mentioned, but this was almost as good.

"What a strange land," said Rolf after a long moment. "So plain, yet it hides such beauty."

Erik agreed silently as he scrambled down the hill after Rolf. The slope was covered in bushes, most not reaching his waist. Birds watched from the brush, flying up when Rolf and Erik grew close.

Only a few minutes after throwing his line in the river, Rolf pulled out a striped olive-green fish. He killed and cleaned it, then gathered twigs and small branches for a fire. Erik watched curiously as Rolf drove half a dozen forked twigs into the ground around his fire, then cut the cleaned fish in half. He wove the fish onto sticks and propped them on the forked twigs so they hung over the fire.

Feeling a tug on his rod, Erik found himself wrestling with his own catch. Twice he thought he'd lose it, but after several minutes he landed a large, spotted green fish, its mouth full of pointed teeth.

"A pike," said Rolf with satisfaction. "We had pike in Norway. What we can't eat now and for breakfast, we'll smoke."

Erik smashed a rock onto the wriggling fish, crushing its head. He cleaned it and dropped it into the pail. Picking up his rod, he caught one more fish before the supper was cooked.

The fish made the best meal Erik had eaten in weeks – if not forever.

They walked home in the cool of the evening, the long shadows from the setting sun stretching ahead of them. Erik filleted the fish, putting them to soak in salted water overnight. Rolf dug around in their scraps of wood and built an improvised smokehouse over a shallow hole in the ground.

Erik dragged a bench outside and sat on it, leaning against the sod wall. One by one, stars appeared. In the distance an animal howled.

Erik had never seen a sky so wide.

They ate fried fish for breakfast the next morning, then Erik put the rest of the fish to smoke. Afterwards he helped Rolf with the outhouse. They had wood for the seat and the frame, but used the canvas for walls and a roof.

"I guess we can't move again," Erik said, handing Rolf the last section of canvas.

Rolf looked at Erik, his eyebrows raised.

"Nothing to cover the wagon with."

"That's right," said Rolf. His eyes rested briefly on the posts Olaf had dug into the ground. "We're here to stay."

That evening Rolf filled his jacket pockets with flat-bread and *gjetost*.

"I'll walk to Lars's in the morning," he said, "then take his horses to Hanley. It'll be quicker." He met Erik's eyes, then looked away. "I'll need you to stay here and tend to the animals."

Disappointed, Erik nodded, saying nothing.

When morning came it was windy and cool. Erik watched Rolf set off across the prairie. He dropped to the ground, leaning against the house, feeling it solid and warm against his back. He watched a hawk swoop through the air, nearly touching the ground as it picked up a rodent. The oxen grazed nearby while Tess and her calf dozed by the slough. The chickens were scattered around the yard, scratching for insects.

Flat and unfriendly, that's what the country felt like. Flat and unfriendly and lonely. It had been lonely enough when Rolf was there. It was worse when he was gone.

But he couldn't sit all day. If they were going to live in this place, he'd have to make it work. They needed a garden patch for vegetables. Erik jumped to his feet and grabbed the spade. As he dug, he occasionally glanced at the grazing oxen, wishing he was strong enough to hold the plough in the ground.

The soil was hard and dry, the digging difficult. After a while, Erik set the spade aside and walked east. As he walked he was aware of rises and falls, but after the mountains of Norway he couldn't call it anything but flat.

No matter which way he looked, everything was the same.

How easy it would be to get lost.

Lost.

Heart thumping, Erik swung around.

There it was, in the distance, the sod house, small, brown, hugging the ground.

After that Erik looked back often.

He saw survey stakes in the corners of their quarter and caught a glimpse of a building further east. In a hollow he found an almost dry slough, thick with grass. Bushes grew along one side, some of them taller than Erik. As he approached, birds flew out, clutching berries in their beaks. Erik ate some of the purple berries, finding them juicy and sweet.

In the distance he could see a wolf walking across the prairie. No, not a wolf. It was too small. A dog, maybe.

Erik set off after it. The animal turned away, breaking into a run. Not a dog.

Hungry, Erik headed back to the sod house. He checked that the chickens were still alive, then heated a tin of beans. After eating, he used the pickaxe to break up the hard sod of the garden, but looked around often in case the wolf-dog returned.

By the fourth day, Erik knew their quarter section almost as well as he knew his grandfather's farm in Norway. He spent the morning digging in the garden, then loaded one of the water barrels onto the wagon.

The oxen stood quietly while he fumbled with the yoke.

"You're not horses," said Erik, patting Black's neck, "but for oxen you're not bad."

CHAPTER SEVEN

Reunited

When Erik returned to the sod house with the barrel of spring water, the door stood open. He jumped down from the wagon just as his mother stepped outside. She caught him in a hug.

"Ma!" exclaimed Erik "You're here!"

"We arrived about an hour ago," she said. "Rolf just left to return the horses and wagon to Lars. How are you? Rolf tells me you've been working hard."

"There's much to do," Erik said uncomfortably. "How – how do you like the house?"

"I was glad to get out of the wind."

"We filled all the cracks so the wind couldn't get inside," Erik said quickly, noticing she hadn't said she liked the house. And how could she? It was made of dirt.

He dipped most of the water from the barrel on the wagon to the barrel by the door, then carried the last pail inside. An embroidered cloth covered the wooden table and there were shelves against one wall. Elsa was arranging wildflowers in a cup.

"Did you see my hen?" she asked eagerly.

"The chickens are all over," he said. "I see them every day."

"Not those chickens!" Elsa ran to the door. "Come, little hen," she cooed. "Come here."

A chicken pecking the ground near the tent ran toward Elsa, who dropped a few kernels of corn on the ground.

"She knows me."

"She knows the corn," said Erik. "Did you get this hen to replace the one that died in Hanley?"

"She didn't die," Elsa said indignantly. She knelt down and smoothed the glossy brown feathers. "She was sick, but I made her better."

Erik went to move the wagon, leaving Elsa trying to making friends with one of the other hens.

His mother watched as he tethered the oxen. "I need you to start milking the cow again."

Erik stared at her. Though he'd milked Tess when they first bought her, she hadn't been milked since they'd left Minnesota.

"The calf drinks all the milk. Tess won't let me milk her."

"Then you'll have to separate them, won't you?"

It sounded so easy. And it might be if they had a barn or corral.

Erik met Rolf when he walked into the yard after returning the horses.

"I was wondering," said Erik, "while we still have Mr. Johnson's sod-cutting plough, if we should make a shed."

"A shed?" repeated Rolf.

"Ma wants me to milk the cow," said Erik. "If we lock

her up for the night so the calf can't drink, Tess might let me milk her in the morning."

"Oh."

"And we could store things in the shed, too, like chicken feed and tools."

"I wanted to start breaking land," said Rolf, "but I guess it can wait a few days."

They marked off the site for the shed that evening and began cutting sods in the morning.

"We'll have lots of food," Elsa told Erik over flatbread and soup at noon. "Today we planted asparagus and rhubarb and potatoes and onions, and even a baby apple tree that Mama brought from Norway."

"It's the middle of July," her mother said. "That's late to be planting a garden."

"It will rain," Elsa said confidently, "and everything will grow fast."

Erik hoped she was right. It hadn't rained since the day after he and Rolf left Hanley, and the ground he'd dug was dry and hard.

"To be sure, we'll ask God to bless our garden," Inga said, "He knows we need food for the winter."

After supper, Erik saw that his mother wasn't waiting for the rain, but carrying the dishwater out to sprinkle on the seeds.

Three evenings later, Erik closed Tess into the new shed. In the house, Inga was heating water.

"Tomorrow is Sunday," she said, "and we're going to

church. Tonight we'll all have baths."

"Sunday?" repeated Erik "Church?" Then it hit him. "Baths?" In a one-room house?

Inga had Erik hang a blanket in the corner by the stove, then pour water into the washtub behind it. Elsa had the first bath. Inga added more hot water to the tub, then disappeared behind the blanket.

When she came out, she pointed to the dish by the tub. "Don't forget to use the soap," she told Erik, "and dry your feet well so you don't turn the floor to mud."

Erik sighed and emptied the kettle into the tub. He added more buffalo chips to the fire, then refilled the kettle to heat water for Rolf.

The next morning there was no sunshine on the tent when Erik woke. The canvas whipped in the breeze and heavy clouds hung low in the sky. Erik grabbed a pail from the house and went to see if Tess would let him milk her.

The calf was standing outside the shed, bawling. Erik shoved it out of the way and slipped into the shed.

In the dim light from the small openings they'd left in the walls, Erik steered the cow into a corner. He slipped the pail beneath her and dropped onto a short-legged stool.

"That's a good girl," he said, trying to sound soothing. "Just give me a bit of milk, and I'll let you out with your baby."

Tess didn't want to stand still. She flicked her tail and moved her feet restlessly, then walked to the door. There were only a few centimetres of milk in the bottom of Erik's pail.

He tethered Tess, then hurried to eat breakfast. A Norwegian travelling pastor was speaking at a school some distance away. Lars was picking them up for the church service and picnic afterwards.

"Olaf isn't with you?" Inga asked when the wagon pulled up by the sod house. "I wanted to meet him."

"You will," said Lars. "He rode one of the horses."

"Even though he says they're all too big and slow," added Aunt Kirsten. "He wants to be a cowboy like some of his friends."

"Nonsense," said Lars. "He doesn't know what he's saying. He's young yet."

Bumping along in the back of the wagon, Erik wished he was riding a horse, even a slow one.

Church was held inside the school. Afterwards, despite threatening weather, everyone spread blankets on the grass. Kirsten and Inga unpacked their baskets together. The meats, fresh bread and desserts looked like a feast to Erik.

His plate was almost empty when a shadow fell across his face. A pair of long legs stood beside him.

"Olaf," exclaimed Kirsten, smiling warmly, "I thought you'd forgotten to eat."

"Have you ever seen that boy forget to eat?" Lars was smiling, but Erik thought his voice sounded strained.

"I have your favourite turnovers," Kirsten began. "But first I want you to meet –"

"Inga," interrupted Rolf, his face red above his beard. "My wife Inga and her daughter Elsa." Setting his tin mug on the blanket, he stood before continuing.

"Inga, this is my son, Olaf."

Elsa glanced at Erik, her face showing her surprise, but Inga rose quickly to her feet. "Olaf," she exclaimed warmly, throwing her arms around him. "I'm so glad to meet you. Rolf talks of you often."

He does?

When Olaf pulled away from Inga's hug, his face was as flushed as Rolf's.

Kirsten filled a plate for Olaf. He took it, mumbling his thanks, and moved away. Erik wished he had the courage to join him.

When they finished eating, Lars and Kirsten took Inga and Rolf to meet some of the other people. Erik scanned the crowd, hoping for someone close to his own age.

Seeing mostly adults and young children, he gave up and reached for another piece of Kirsten's saskatoon pie.

"For a skinny kid, you sure can eat."

"Hello, Olaf," said Erik, wondering if he was eating too much. "Did you want some pie?"

"I can get it myself." He crouched down and transferred a generous slice to his plate, then glanced at Erik.

"You got that farm of yours all built now?" he asked, his voice challenging.

"We built a sod shed," said Erik. "And a hutch for the chickens. We haven't started breaking land."

"Got any horses?"

Erik bit his lip. Olaf knew they didn't have horses.

"We've got good oxen," Erik said at last. "They don't head straight for sloughs or ignore our directions, not like some I've heard about."

Olaf grunted and forked up a bite of the pie.

"I didn't know Rolf had a son," Erik said in a rush. "Not till the other day."

"So that was a lie, then," said Olaf. "When your mother said he talks about me."

"I guess Rolf talks to her, just not to me and Elsa." Olaf's fork paused as Erik spoke. "Rolf doesn't talk to me much at all. We just work all the time."

"But he's your father now." Erik wasn't sure if it was a question or a statement.

"No, he's not," said Erik. "Elsa calls him Papa sometimes, but she doesn't remember our own father."

"And you do?"

"He drowned when I was three," said Erik. "I only remember bits."

Olaf shot Erik a sharp glance. He opened his mouth to speak, just as someone called his name.

"Hey, Hanson! Time for baseball."

A man ran up to them, pretending to hit Olaf with a wooden bat. Another man strolled behind him, tossing a small white ball in the air. "We're getting up a game," he said to Erik. "You want to play?"

Olaf jumped to his feet, swallowing the last bite of his pie. Erik, who'd heard of baseball but never seen it played, said he'd watch for a while. He followed the men over to the playing field, wishing they hadn't been interrupted, wondering what Olaf was going to say.

Olaf's first turn at bat got him to third base, but he wasn't able to make it home. His next turn was accompanied by loud thunder and a sprinkling of rain.

The pitcher threw the ball; Olaf swung and missed.

The rain came down harder and most of the spectators ran for the school. Erik didn't move.

The pitcher threw the ball again. Olaf hit it with a loud crack. He started running; at the same time it started to hail. Erik pulled the brim of his hat down over his eyes and ran toward the school.

He saw Rolf and Elsa in the crowd ahead of him with the blankets and picnic basket. Olaf was one of the last into the building, laughing as he wiped the rain from his face with a handkerchief.

Minutes later someone looked out the door.

"The shower's over," he said. "Let's finish our game."

"Great," called Olaf from the back of the room. "I got a home run."

"Doesn't count when you're the only one still playing."

Lars tapped Erik on the shoulder. "We're going before it rains again."

Erik watched the men hurrying back to the baseball field.

"Maybe you can play next time," said Elsa.

"It doesn't matter," said Erik roughly. He brushed past Elsa and climbed into the wagon.

Other people prepared to leave as well. Erik watched enviously as they hitched up horses. No one had come to the picnic with oxen.

The schoolyard was only damp from the shower, but as they neared home, Erik could see it had rained more. There was water pooled in low spots along the trail and in the yard. Hailstones lay by the sod house.

Erik jumped down from the wagon, scooping up a handful of the frozen white pebbles.

"Big enough to break the stems on plants," said Lars.

"Good thing our garden is still in the ground," said Elsa.

"That's right, Elsa," said Inga. "For us, it's just moisture to help the plants grow."

"Likely damaged some crops," said Rolf.

Erik looked at the stones melting in his hand. There was so much about farming that they couldn't control.

He tossed the hailstones to the ground. The chickens pecked at them, expecting grain.

CHAPTER EIGHT

Snared!

Monday morning, Erik followed rabbit tracks through the wet soil of the garden but lost them in the grass. He found more tracks in the brush around the slough.

Going into the house, Erik dug through one of the trunks.

"What are you looking for?" asked Elsa.

"Wire," said Erik. "Thin wire. I think I can snare us some meat."

"Rabbits!" exclaimed Elsa immediately. "The boys in Minnesota snared rabbits. Can I help?"

"Only if you get up very early," said Erik. He unwound the wire, feeling its strength. "I'm going out before it's light so I can catch one as soon as it gets up."

The song of the birds woke Erik before dawn. In the still darkness, he took his loop of wire and headed for the slough. He'd only taken a few steps when something bounded out of the grass ahead of him.

A rabbit already? Weren't they supposed to be sleeping?

Erik arranged his wire loop along a path he'd chosen the day before and lay down close by, holding the end of the wire. He tried to stay motionless, but the ground was damp and biting insects whined around his face, stinging him repeatedly. He cautiously reached up with his left hand to brush them away. One bit the finger of his right hand, and he jerked it without thinking. He felt the snare tighten on empty air, just as the plants around him rustled. Had a rabbit passed and he'd missed it?

Erik had no idea. He reset his snare and lay down again. It was getting lighter now. There were rustles in the bushes all around him. He held his breath as a large shadow appeared. It moved and became a deer, followed by a fawn. Erik raised his head as the deer stepped carefully through the plants in front of him. When it moved out of sight, Erik sat up and peered around a bush. The two animals bent their heads to drink at the slough.

At breakfast, Elsa asked if Erik had caught any rabbits.

He shook his head, not pausing as he ate his porridge.

"Did you see some?"

"*Ja,*" he said shortly.

"So will you try again tomorrow?"

"There must be a better way. I'll think about it."

"Can you think about it while you get water from the spring?" asked his mother.

Rolf set his cup down and looked at Inga. "Are you out of water?" he asked. "I was going to start breaking land today."

"We used so much having baths and washing the dirt from travelling off the dishes," said Inga. "Maybe we can use the slough water for a couple of days."

Erik shook his head. Not for drinking. He and Rolf

drank from the slough when they first arrived, but it tasted worse now.

"Do you think I could borrow horses from Uncle Lars to get water from the spring?" he asked. "It wouldn't take very long."

Rolf sighed. "We need a well," he said.

"You can't do everything at once," said Inga. "We'll find a way."

"I can get two barrels this time," suggested Erik.

"I'll use slough water for washing," said Inga, "so the spring water will last longer."

Rolf nodded slowly. "You can walk over to Lars's and ask him," he said to Erik. "Maybe they need water and you could bring some for all of us."

"Can I go, too?" asked Elsa.

On their walk across the prairie, Erik kept his eyes open for rabbits. He saw only one, but many of the brown, whistling rodents. He wondered if anyone ever ate them.

Kirsten met them at the door, her hands covered in flour.

"How nice to see you," she greeted them. "I'm up to my arms in bread dough, trying to make German bread."

"You mean like Mrs. Haugen makes?" asked Elsa eagerly. "I helped her when we stayed there."

"Then you should help me."

"Is Uncle Lars here?" asked Erik. "I wondered, I mean Rolf wondered, if I could use your horses to get water from the spring. Do you need water, too?"

"We always need water." His aunt smiled as she went

back to her bowl of dough. "Lars and Olaf are stacking lumber in the back. Why don't you go and talk to them?"

"I'll just stay here for now," said Elsa.

"You can find an apron on the shelf behind me," said Kirsten.

Erik closed the door and headed around the house.

"Are you used to driving horses?" Lars asked when Erik made his request. "Perhaps Olaf should go with you. He knows our team."

Erik felt his face turn red. "I don't want to interrupt your work," he said. "I helped my grandfather with his horses in Norway."

"I'm sure you did," said Lars, "but we need water anyway. Olaf, load the barrels on the stoneboat and you can go together. It'll be quicker with two."

Olaf harnessed two horses to the flat, runnerless sled. Erik rolled on one barrel, finding it easier than lifting the barrel onto the wagon. Olaf rolled on the other barrel, then went into the house. He returned a moment later with a metal pail and a rifle. Turning the pail upside down on the stoneboat, he plopped himself down on it, laid the rifle between the barrels and picked up the reins.

"Let's go," he said.

Erik jumped on, balancing himself between the water barrels as they bumped out of the yard. It was his first experience with a stoneboat. He hoped both he and the barrels would stay on.

"Here," said Olaf suddenly. "Hold these!"

Erik let go of the barrels and grabbed the reins. Olaf

relaxed on his upside-down pail and Erik found himself driving the horses.

They picked up two barrels at the sod house, along with another pail. Olaf held the reins as they set off across country to the spring. This time Erik sat on a pail, too.

"Rolf would like to dig a well," he said, trying to make conversation.

Olaf nodded.

"But how will he know where there's water?" Erik went on.

"I expect he won't."

"That's a lot of work without knowing you'll reach water in the end."

"Heard of a man in Minnesota who dug fifteen wells without finding water."

Erik stared at Olaf. Fifteen wells!

He considered that for several silent minutes, not speaking again till a rabbit bounded out of the grass ahead of them.

"I tried to snare a rabbit this morning."

"How many snares did you set?"

"Just one," said Erik, puzzled. "That's all I could hold at once."

Olaf glanced at Erik sideways. "You might try the sort you don't have to hold. You can set more than one and you don't have to wait around."

Erik was thinking about how to set a snare to tighten on its own, when Olaf stopped the horses and shoved the reins into his hands.

"Hold them still," said Olaf. He reached back for the

rifle, then stepped off the stoneboat and moved sound-lessly a few feet away. Dropping to his knees, he aimed toward the spring and pulled the trigger.

Several brown, chicken-like birds lifted off the ground. Some flew into the bushes by the spring, others fluttered across the prairie.

The horses started at the sound of the rifle. Erik pulled hard on the reins to keep the horses from moving.

"Let 'em go." Olaf walked beside the horses, stooping to pick up a dead bird.

"They make good eating," he said, dropping it onto the stoneboat.

"What are they?"

"I call them wild chickens." Olaf nodded to Erik. "You did a good job with the horses." He set the rifle down and picked up his pail.

The trip back with the full barrels was slower, but the stoneboat moved more smoothly. They dropped two barrels off at the sod house, then Erik drove on with Olaf to get Elsa.

After unloading the water, Olaf got a piece of wire about a half-metre long. "I snared rabbits in Minnesota," he said. "Now I shoot them, but it's more expensive, especially if you miss." He made a small loop at one end of the wire, pulled the other end through, then made a loop at that end. The resulting circle was big enough for a rabbit's head to slip through easily.

"Rabbits are most active at night," Olaf said as he tied a string onto the second small loop, "so check your snares each morning or a coyote might get the rabbit first."

"Coyotes look like small wolves?" guessed Erik.

"That's right," said Olaf. "Watch your chickens. They'll eat them, too."

He dug a large stick firmly into the ground and tied the string to it. "When the rabbit gets caught, it struggles. The string tied to this stick is what makes the snare tighten." He used a couple of smaller sticks to hold the snare open and in place.

"Understand?" asked Olaf. At Erik's nod, he removed the sticks and tossed the snare to Erik. "Find a good spot to set it."

Erik set three snares that day. In the morning they were all empty, though one had been sprung.

After resetting the trap, he took the milk pail into the shed. Tess still refused to stand still. He had to find a way to tie her in place, but today his concern was finding grass. When he looked around, the grass was eaten to the ground on every side of the house.

Rolf, leading the oxen to the plough, glanced at Erik. "Is there a problem?" he asked.

"Ja," said Erik. "There's no more grass, not close by."

"So we just tether the animals further away."

"Maybe," said Erik tentatively. "Maybe we don't need to tether them."

Rolf looked at him blankly.

"We could just let them roam on their own," said Erik. "They should come back here for water."

"But what if they don't? Or if they're far away when

we need them?"

"We can try it first with Tess," said Erik, knowing he would be the one searching if the cow didn't return.

"Fine." Rolf lifted the yoke over the oxen's heads. "We need to put up hay for the winter," he said. "You can cut grass while I break land."

Erik nodded, then led the cow to the slough and slipped the rope off her neck. "Don't get lost," he said warningly. "We want your milk."

Back at the shed, Erik dragged the scythe outside. It was a large tool with a long curved blade and a wooden handle. Two handgrips stuck out of the handle at right angles, one at the top, one about halfway down.

Erik sharpened the blade with a whetstone. Taking both the scythe and the whetstone, he set off for the slough with the saskatoon bushes.

Though he'd never used a scythe, Erik knew how it was supposed to work. He swung it from the right to the left, trying to skim above the ground, leaving a tidy swath by his side.

Whump! The scythe dug into the soil, coming to an abrupt halt. Erik tried again, missing the ground, but cutting taller than he wanted. He swung one more time, glad no one was watching.

Whack! The scythe hit a half-buried stone.

Erik dropped the scythe and threw himself on the grass.

He looked up at the sky. The same sky he'd seen over Norway, he thought. It was still there over his grandparents.

The world seemed smaller suddenly.

After a while he picked up the scythe. He sharpened

the blade again and went back to mowing.

After he cut the last strip of standing grass, he looked at the slough. All that work, and so little hay. They were going to need much more to feed four animals all winter.

The next morning Erik found a dead rabbit in one of the snares. He moved the other two to new spots and set them all again.

"Look what Erik has," said Elsa when Erik brought the rabbit to the house.

"That will make a good meal," Inga said. "Thank you, Erik."

"Where shall I put it?" he asked.

"After you skin and clean it," his mother said, "hang it in the shade till I'm ready to cook it."

Erik stared at his mother. He'd hoped she would clean and skin the rabbit.

Elsa grinned and handed Erik a sharp knife. He went outside, crouching down behind the house. He could do this, he told himself. Just like all the other new things he'd done since coming to this empty land. He could do this.

Afterwards, Erik scrubbed his hands in the basin and went to cut more hay. Rolf was off to the east, breaking prairie. He did as much as he could each day, whatever the weather. Erik thought he would plough all day if the oxen could work that long.

A few days later, it was drizzling outside when Erik checked his snares. He brought two rabbits into the house, skinned and cleaned.

"Manga takk," said his mother. "They're nice and plump, aren't they? Please cut them in pieces for me, Erik."

Cut them up! Cleaning was bad enough, but cutting them was women's work!

Angrily, Erik knocked a bug off the table, grinding it into the dirt.

"Can't you do it?" asked Inga, giving him a surprised look.

Elsa touched his arm. "I'll show you how," she said. "It's not hard."

Erik glared at her, then at his mother, but neither seemed to care. "Thanks, Elsa," said Inga, turning back to the sock she was darning.

Afterwards, Erik dug a hole in the shed ready for a branch or tree trunk to use for a post. He hoped tying Tess to it would keep her from moving so much when he milked her.

When he came out of the shed, the sun had come out. Rolf stood between the house and the slough looking at the ground.

"We're going to dig a well," said Rolf. "Right here."

"How do we do it?" Erik asked.

"With a pick and a spade. When it gets too deep to throw the dirt out, I'll put it in a pail and you'll pull it up with a rope. Then we'll build walls inside the well to keep it from caving in."

Erik didn't know what to say. Digging the garden had been difficult enough.

"Since our slough hasn't dried up like most of the

others," said Rolf, "I'm hoping there's underground water here."

Erik watched Rolf push the spade into the ground.

And thought of the man who dug fifteen wells without getting water.

CHAPTER NINE

Trees

One day in August, Erik took a different route to the river, further north than he'd gone before. Some of the land he crossed was native prairie, but other pieces had been broken and seeded to grain, now turning from green to gold.

Further on, he found himself at the edge of a cliff. Looking down, he saw, not the river, but a small valley with more hills on the other side. Where the hills met, someone had built a corral and a small wooden building.

Erik thought the corral was big enough for forty or fifty animals, but it held only two horses. There were no people in sight.

He cast one longing glance at the horses, then headed south along the top of the cliff. He finally reached the river by the same route he'd gone in the past.

Other times when he'd come to fish, he'd hurried back to work, but today it was too hot to cut hay and Rolf was gone. He was building a granary with Mr. Johnson in return for borrowing his sod-cutting plough.

That meant Erik could finally do what he'd wanted to do ever since Gunnar Haugen had mentioned the valley of the trees.

He placed his rod and pail under a bush and walked south. He followed the river for a while, then moved further up the bank. The brush soon gave way to trees – real trees that towered over his head.

The ground felt spongy under his feet from years of fallen leaves. Erik's heart beat faster. It was just like the forests in Norway!

He grabbed a branch and pulled himself up into one of the trees. Stretching for the next branch, and the one after that, he climbed till the branches were too small to hold his weight.

The tree swayed as he gazed about. Through the leaves, he caught glimpses of the river to the west, but just the face of a cliff to the east.

After several minutes he half-slid, half-climbed down the tree, dropping the last couple of metres. He lost his footing and tumbled, unhurt, to the ground. Right beside his face was a miniature tree, twenty centimetres tall, its leaves huge on its stem-like trunk. Erik dug through the decayed leaves with his hands, freeing the tree's roots. He found another close by and slipped both inside his shirt.

After wandering through the trees for a few minutes, Erik found himself among shrubs and grass again. He walked around the perimeter of the trees, amazed that a forest, even a small one, could exist next to so much flat prairie.

With an eye on the sun, Erik went back to his fishing rod. He cast, then leaned against a rock, watching the birds on the water.

A sharp pull on the line almost caused Erik to drop his rod. Clutching it tightly, he hung on as the fish jerked and pulled. He dug his heels into the ground, determined not to let go. Suddenly, the line went slack and Erik fell to the ground.

Close to the shore, a huge pike jumped high above the water, the sun glistening on its scales.

Erik tied a new hook to his line but just caught two small fish before climbing back up to the prairie.

The grass where he usually walked had been flattened. Further on, Erik could see that while he was in the valley, animals had cut across a field of grain, breaking the stalks.

Cattle? Erik wondered, or maybe one last herd of buffalo. Squatting down, he looked closely at the tracks.

Horseshoes! But who would ride through a field of grain?

They'd been travelling north, Erik saw. One day he'd follow their trail to see if they went to the corral.

At home he planted the trees in front of the sod house while Inga fried the fish.

"This is so good," Elsa said, taking a second piece.

"Our meals have improved," agreed Inga. "I'm glad we have a hunter and fisherman in the family." Erik glanced at Rolf, hoping he would say something, but he ate without comment.

The next morning the wind was blowing when Erik crawled out of the tent. He fetched the milk pail from the house, then slipped into the shed to milk Tess.

She surprised Erik by standing quietly – until the calf bawled outside the door. Her head jerked and her rope-like tail switched, hitting him right in the face with a dirty, stinging slap.

Erik looked at the pail clutched between his knees, half full of the foamy milk. He wanted to quit right then. Let Tess out. The calf could have the rest.

But if he did that, the cow would win.

Clenching his teeth, Erik reached for the udder and squeezed the way his grandfather had taught him long ago in Norway. A stream of milk shot into the pail.

"I can do this," he muttered, squeezing again. "I can do this."

His mother was making breakfast when Erik brought the milk into the house. She smiled as she handed him a clean cloth to lay over the pail.

"You're such a good helper, Erik," she said smiling. "Your father would be so proud of you."

Erik dropped onto the bench by the table, surprised to hear her mention his father. She hardly ever did, especially since marrying Rolf.

He picked up a piece of the heavy dark bread and gazed at it sightlessly. Would his father be proud of him? Or would he take all his work for granted, like Rolf? How could he ever know?

"What are you going to do today?" Inga asked.

Erik shook his head slightly and reached for the butter. Butter they wouldn't have if he didn't milk Tess.

"Look for more winter feed, I guess."

The door opened and Rolf came in along with a gust

of wind that lifted dust on the floor. Inga poured him a cup of coffee and sat down at the table.

"I saw Lars yesterday," said Rolf. "He was just back with a load of lumber from Hanley." He took a sip of his coffee and wiped his mouth with the back of his hand. "The auction sale is only a couple weeks away, and he wants to be ready."

"Auction sale?" repeated Elsa. "Are they auctioning the wood?"

"Don't you remember what Mr. Haugen told us?" said Erik. "They're selling the business lots in Green Valley at the end of August. Uncle Lars is hoping the people who buy lots will buy his wood, too."

"I thought Olaf was doing the hauling," said Inga.

"Apparently he found something else to fill his days," said Rolf. His voice was stiff.

Erik left to get the oxen, wondering what it felt like to have a son who wouldn't talk to you.

When he stepped outside, the first thing he saw was Tess standing in the garden, carrot tops hanging from her mouth.

"You stupid cow!" Erik yelled, tearing toward her. Up till now she'd run loose without a problem, always coming back to drink at the slough, but he wasn't surprised the garden had caught her eye. It was the greenest place around, even though the plants were still small. They'd eaten a few carrots as Inga thinned them, and one day they'd had fresh potatoes, but the vegetables needed weeks of sunshine to get full-sized. Rain wouldn't hurt, either.

Tess turned and ran into the prairie, stumbling over the uneven ground Rolf had broken. Erik let her go, but the next time he had her, she was going to be tethered like the oxen, though he'd be walking a long way to do it. He got the oxen from where he'd tethered them on the other side of the quarter and led them to the slough.

Nearby, Rolf was building a tripod over the well hole.

"This will make it easier to bring up the dirt," he said. Erik nodded. They'd been working on the well in odd moments between other jobs, but progress was slow. This pulley should speed things up somewhat. Now they just needed something to make the digging easier.

Rolf yoked the oxen to the plough while Erik watered his trees. The leaves on one were wilted and drooping, but the other stood straight and strong, as if it had never been moved.

Picking up the scythe, Erik headed west, toward the river, looking for grass that no one else was claiming. He found a small patch at the bottom of a hill and cut it swiftly. Leaving it to dry, he moved on looking for another patch.

The sound of hoofbeats caused him to swing around. Two horses and riders cantered toward him. One pulled to a stop a short distance away, the other rode in a circle around Erik, stopping right in front of him.

"Hi, there, walking boy," exclaimed Olaf in English.

Erik stepped back instinctively, then stretched his hand out to pat the horse's neck.

"Is this your horse, Olaf?" he asked, sticking with Norwegian. "He's beautiful." The horse was all black, except for a blaze on his forehead and the raw skin of the fresh Boxed Q brand.

"Unfortunately not," said Olaf. "One day I'll have my own horse, but these belong to Pete. Jim and I are just trying them out."

Erik greeted Jim. The man with Olaf looked at home on the horse in his wide-brimmed grey hat, cowboy boots and leather chaps. Jim nodded at Erik without speaking. Pulling a pouch from his jacket pocket, he rolled a cigarette.

"I heard you're not hauling lumber anymore," said Erik, turning back to Olaf. "Are you working for the man who owns these horses?"

"*Ja,* I work for Pete some. I was tired of driving to Hanley and back."

Erik stared at Olaf. Tired of driving to Hanley? Erik was tired of working, too, but he didn't have a choice. What would Ma say if he told her he hated cutting grass?

"We best be gettin' back," said Jim. He lit his cigarette, then snuffed the burning match between his thumb and index finger. Turning his horse around, he dropped the dead match at Erik's feet.

As Olaf followed Jim across the prairie, Erik recalled the cowboys he'd seen in Hanley. One had been older, with a dark, drooping moustache. And the other? He'd had a wispy, brown beard, Erik remembered, and the older man had called him Jim. If he shaved off that beard, he'd look just like the man with Olaf.

CHAPTER TEN

Sold!

Throughout the night before the Green Valley land sale, rain drummed against the tent. Erik dreamed he was swimming and woke to find his feet in a puddle of water. After piling his bedding in the centre of the tent, he ran to get the milk pail, dodging raindrops all the way.

Erik's mother and Rolf were at the table when he brought the milk into the house. Erik filled the water pail from the barrel outside the door, then came back in, shaking rain from his hair. His mother handed him a towel, then poured him a cup of coffee.

"You better eat," she said. "Lars will be picking you up soon."

"I want to go, too," said Elsa.

She was curled up on a straw-stuffed mattress, watching them.

"Ah, you wouldn't be any help," said Erik. "Uncle Lars needs someone who can pile lumber."

"It's raining outside," Inga reminded Elsa, shaking her head. As she spoke a drop of water dripped from the roof onto the table. Erik glanced up and saw another drop hanging on the edge of the tarpaper, ready to fall.

Inga set a bowl to catch the drips. The sod roof always leaked when it rained for more than a couple of hours.

"I'm sorry for the men sleeping in tents at the townsite," said Rolf.

"I slept in a tent last night," Erik reminded him. Trust Rolf to sympathize with strangers rather than his own stepson.

"Were you cold?" asked Elsa. "Did you get wet?"

"Rain came in at the edges."

"Bring your bedding in here to stay dry," suggested his mother.

Erik glanced at the pool of muddy water accumulating in the dish. "It'll be all right."

"I'm coming to the townsite later," said Rolf. "Lars asked me to help him for a few days." He chewed thoughtfully on a piece of bread. "Then I'll look for work in town. I expect it will pay better than stooking."

Rolf had stooked for a neighbour for a few days, but instead of cash he'd been paid a roll of barbed wire and two sacks of oats.

Someone pounded on the door. It flew open and Lars and Kirsten stepped inside.

"They're moving my house," said Kirsten with a laugh. "Hope you don't mind if I spend the day with you."

"Of course not," said Inga. She hurried over to take Kirsten's wet coat and hat.

"You ready to go, Erik?" asked Lars. "Olaf has the wagon loaded with lumber and is already on his way to the townsite. As soon as we buy a lot, we'll unload it and go back for more."

"You're moving the building today?" Erik asked.

"*Ja!* I've got Rolf and another fellow lined up for that."

"Is it going to be a store now, Uncle Lars?" asked Elsa.

"That it is. I spent the last few days getting it ready."

"My kitchen has become a long sales counter," said Kirsten. "I tell Lars he has to build a house for me soon. I can only live in a store for so long!"

Erik pulled on his thick jacket and peaked hat and stepped out into the rain. He needed a wide hat like the cowboys wore, he decided, to keep the rain off better. The horses stamped their feet impatiently. Erik greeted them both, then climbed into the buggy and picked up the reins.

When Lars joined Erik, he took the reins with a friendly smile. "I'm glad Rolf brought you along when he came here."

Erik wondered if Rolf felt the same way.

The Green Valley townsite was just east of the valley with the big trees. The last time Erik had gone past, it was still a wheat field, but now the grain was gone and the lots were surveyed and staked.

Erik was amazed at all the tents he saw. Parked beside them were every kind of wagon and buggy and even some automobiles, the first Erik had seen since coming to Canada. The auctioneer stood in a buggy where he could be seen by everyone, giving information about the sale. There were a few boys in the crowd, but Erik couldn't see any women. In the excitement, no one seemed to care about the rain or the mud.

Erik scanned the crowd, looking for a familiar face.

Most of the men looked like businessmen, with long coats over their black suits. The few people he recognized as neighbours looked warmer in their work jackets. Occasionally he heard someone speaking Norwegian, but most of the talk was in English.

"Good morning, Erik. Isn't this a fine day?" Erik felt a hand rest heavily on his shoulders. He glanced up to see Gunnar Haugen. "All ready to buy a lot and start a business?"

Erik grinned back. "I think I'll just watch today."

"You watch us, then," said Mr. Haugen. "We've got some good ones picked out."

The first lots sold for more than Rolf was paying for their hundred and sixty acres. Erik looked anxiously at Lars. Maybe he couldn't afford that much.

Lars wrote something in a notebook. Gunnar Haugen, on his other side, nodded.

A few minutes later they bought two lots, side by side.

Mr. Haugen went to arrange payment in the auctioneer's tent while Lars looked around the crowd. "Where's Olaf?" he asked. "We need to unload that wagon."

Erik ran beside Lars as he strode toward his new lot. Olaf was already there. "I saw you bid," he said, pulling a long timber from the wagon. "I knew you'd want to move quickly." The cowboy, Jim, grabbed the other end of the board.

Lars pulled out a plank. Erik caught the end as it came off the wagon.

Together the four of them unloaded the wagon in minutes. Jim left to see if Pete had bought a lot, while Olaf and Lars climbed onto the wagon seat.

Lars looked at Erik. "You coming along?" he asked.

Erik climbed into the wagon box, kneeling behind the seat. Now that the rain had stopped, he hoped the sun would come out and dry his clothes.

Gunnar Haugen waved as they drove away. "Hurry back," he said. "I should have this all sold by then."

"What are you going to do with the land where you've been living?" Erik asked.

"It's not mine," said Lars. "I just rented the land for a few months. We wanted to be close to town so we could do what we're doing right now."

"Move your building as soon as you bought a lot?" asked Erik.

"*Ja,* and sell lumber as soon as people want to buy it."

On the way they met two wagons loaded with lumber. "It looks like other people had the same idea," said Erik. "Maybe there will be no one to buy your wood."

"Not everyone hauled their own lumber from Hanley. We'll sell it all, you'll see."

Up ahead, Erik saw a building where there hadn't been one before. Fascinated, he watched it move toward them, seeming to float over the prairie. As it drew closer, he wasn't surprised to see it was Lars's house, pulled by six oxen. Rolf walked beside the building and a man Erik didn't know walked by the oxen. The last two oxen were Black and Socks.

Heavy ropes stretched between the skids and the oxen.

"This is what I like to see!" exclaimed Lars. "Hardworking men."

"Don't tell us you didn't buy a lot!" Rolf called back.

"Don't worry, we have two!" Lars replied. "They're in

the northeast corner. Gunnar is there."

"Oxen move too slow," said Olaf as they drove past.

"But they're strong," Erik defended them.

When Lars, Olaf and Erik got back to town with a second load of lumber, the house was in its spot, looking just like the store it was now going to be. Erik looked proudly at the building, the first in the new town of Green Valley.

The auction was over, but people still milled around, ignoring their wet clothes. Builders laid out lumber on some of the lots. The ring of hammers was heard from several directions. The lumber Erik had helped stack earlier was gone. Some of it might already be part of a new building, he decided, liking the thought.

He reached to help Olaf unload the second wagonload just as a stranger laid his hand on the board. "We're building today," he said. "I need to buy this whole load."

A man talking to Mr. Haugen looked up. "Sorry," he said, "I just bought most of it."

"Then I'll take the rest," said the first man.

Olaf stopped unloading and leaned against the wagon. "So where do we put the lumber?" He grinned at Erik. "No reason to load it again if we don't have to."

Lars hired Erik for several days to watch the store while he and Mr. Haugen built a lean-to onto the back of the former house. Olaf and Rolf worked non-stop, hauling the lumber piled outside town to the new lumberyard. Olaf drove Lars's wagon and horses while Rolf used his own wagon and oxen. When they drove into the yard, Erik joined them outside to help unload.

Aunt Kirsten was in the store, too, but she hung sheets to divide the space so she could spin or bake out of sight of the customers. "I'm not going to live in a lumber shop," she told Erik. Erik knew his mother would have said the same thing, but he liked the smell of the sawdust and the look of the milled lumber.

He sold other supplies, too, almost anything people needed to build. He counted change from the big wooden cash register and weighed nails. Every time a customer walked into the store, he practiced his English and learned new words.

Most of the people Erik saw were men, though he knew there were women and children on the farms. He expected the men would bring their families to Green Valley when the businesses were built.

One day Kirsten sent Erik to the general store for eggs, giving him a chance to walk through the town. The store was in a tent, run by a Norwegian named Nilson. Erik looked at all the supplies, seeing what he could buy with the twenty-five cents Uncle Lars gave him each day. It would be food for sure, that's what the family needed most. He could buy three tins of pork and beans for fifty cents, but it didn't seem like much for two days' pay. Like the nails he was selling, they were expensive because they were heavy and had to come to Hanley by train and then to Green Valley by wagon. Potatoes might be better. Mr. Nilson sold half a bushel for fifty cents, but Erik wondered if a local farmer would sell for less.

It was hard to believe what he was seeing as he walked

back to the lumberyard. A week ago this was a field, and now it was a town. Wooden buildings rose in every direction, but businesses weren't waiting for them. A bank and a real estate office were working out of tents. An implement shop was almost framed across the street from the lumberyard, and a hotel was going up on the corner. Everyone was working. Even Jim pounded nails on Pete's new livery stable.

Several times a day, Erik stood in front of the lumberyard, watching the town grow. Coming from a country where most of the buildings were old, it was exciting to be part of something so new.

In their hurry to finish, the carpenters kept going after sundown by the light of kerosene torches. At night, when Erik rolled up in a blanket behind the counter in the store, he could see the flickering light of the lamps through the front window, and when he drifted off to sleep it was to the pounding of hammers.

Gunnar Haugen needed to get back to the business in Hanley, so he and Lars worked long days on the lean-to. As soon as the shell was finished, Erik helped move Lars and Kirsten's household belongings into the new rooms.

When all the lumber was transferred to town, Rolf went to work building a drugstore and Olaf returned to hauling lumber from Hanley. With Lars now working in his own store, Erik went back to the farm, bringing with him a bushel of potatoes purchased with his earnings.

Being home seemed very dull after his days in Green Valley.

CHAPTER ELEVEN

Threshing

It was September. In Norway or Minnesota or even Hanley, school was starting, but not for Erik and Elsa.

"We could go to school where we went to church the day it hailed," suggested Elsa.

"It's too far," said Inga. "Even if you took the oxen, it would be more than an hour each way. You'll have to wait till they build a school closer to home."

"What about Green Valley? I could walk there. It's only five kilometres."

"We'll see when they build a school," said Inga, "but it will still be a long walk."

Erik didn't miss sitting in a desk studying numbers and history. He needed school to learn more English and meet boys his age, but it wasn't going to help him with the only thing he wanted to do – farm.

There wasn't time to go to school, anyway. The slough was dry, so Erik had to haul more water. They hadn't worked on the well since before the town auction; Rolf was just too busy. Erik frequently thought of the man who'd dug fifteen dry wells, wondering if Rolf would ever hit water. The well in Green Valley was dug in a spot chosen by a man with a forked stick. They'd found water, so maybe Rolf should have let him choose the location for their well, too.

One day after the garden froze, Erik and Elsa harvested the vegetables, finding small potatoes, short carrots and not much else. With the garden gone, the oxen and cow were allowed to find their own feed. Erik didn't tether them anymore, but sometimes he had to look for them instead. Fortunately, they came back to the yard for water.

He put another post in the shed so he could tie up both Tess and the calf on cold nights, but far enough apart to prevent the calf stealing the milk.

When he wasn't hauling water, Erik searched the river hills for cattle feed and firewood, piling it together, then bringing it back in the wagon. Once he saw horses travelling toward the river. There were three or four riders trailing the herd, all wearing wide-brimmed hats. Erik had learned that cowboys weren't common in farming country. The only ones he'd seen around Green Valley were Jim and two or three others who worked with Pete in his livery stable. It seemed strange that twice now, herds of horses had gone through the area.

The train hadn't reached Green Valley yet, but Erik knew the track was being built from Moose Jaw. It was supposed to reach Green Valley sometime in November.

A couple of times, Lars asked Erik to come to Green Valley with Rolf. Then Erik minded the store while Lars worked on the stable at the back of the lot.

There was always something to see or do in town. Lars had hired a man to bring coal from Hanley, while

Olaf hauled more lumber. Wagons came and went at all hours as other businessmen hauled their supplies from Hanley.

One cool afternoon, Erik was sweeping the floor when he heard rumbles in the street. He poked his head out the door to see three wagons pass by, each piled high with trunks and boxes and household furnishings.

Erik's eyes searched the wagons, looking for boys. The one on a lady's lap was too young, and so were the two crouched behind the driver on the second wagon. But on the third wagon, leaning against a trunk as if he'd come all the way from Norway like that, was a boy who looked just the right age.

Erik waved as the wagon passed in front of him. The boy didn't move but his eyes watched Erik as he passed.

He'll be happy to see me when he learns how few boys are here, thought Erik.

Lars came around the side of the store. "Did you see the wagons?" Erik asked. "It must be the new settlers. I heard Mr. Nilson say there were some coming this fall."

"They might be." Lars started to pull the door closed.

"Can I talk to them?" Erik asked quickly. "I can tell them about the town and where the well is and about there not being a school yet."

"Go along, then." Lars took the broom and Erik dashed out of the store.

"Don't stay too long," his uncle's voice followed him. "Rolf will be here soon."

"I won't," Erik called back over his shoulder.

As he neared the wagons, he saw people gathered to

greet the newcomers. Men shook hands, then turned to help the women down from the wagons. Erik didn't mind that he wouldn't be needed to give information. He just wanted to talk to the boy.

He saw him jump down from the wagon and look toward the buildings, the peak of his cap shading his eyes from the sun.

"Good day," said Erik in Norwegian, running up to him. "Welcome to Green Valley."

The boy looked at Erik, his face totally blank. After a moment he said something unintelligible.

Erik froze. The new settlers weren't from Norway. They weren't even from England. They spoke another language altogether.

The boys looked at each other for a long moment.

Erik smiled and tried again. "Good morning," he said, this time in English.

"Good morning," said the other boy. The words were English, but perhaps he was only imitating Erik.

"My name is Erik. Erik Brekke."

"Colin," said the other boy. "I am Colin O'Brien."

"You speak English," said Erik with relief.

"Yes," said Colin. "And Gaelic."

Erik heard Rolf's voice behind him, then a man from the wagons called for Colin.

"I must go," said both boys at once.

"I'll see you again," said Erik.

Colin held out his hand to Erik. They shook, then he turned and ran back to the wagons. Erik turned to Rolf.

"They speak English and Gaelic. Whatever that is."

"They must be from Scotland or Ireland. They're part of Great Britain."

They usually walked to town, but they'd taken the oxen that day to bring home flour and rice. After climbing onto the wagon, Rolf sat for a moment, staring at the oxen.

"I'm through building for now," he said finally. "I'm joining a threshing crew. It pays better. Your mother, she thinks you're too young and the work will be too hard, but if you want to come along, we'll see if they'll hire you on."

"I'm strong," Erik said, thinking of the sods he'd stacked and the grass he'd cut. "Least I'm as strong as I can be for my size."

"That's right, Erik," said Rolf, "you are, and that's what I told your ma. You've worked hard and you haven't complained. I wouldn't have got near as much done without you."

Erik looked down at his feet. Rolf had never said anything like that to Erik before. It felt good that he'd noticed, just like a real father would.

The thought brought Olaf to mind. Would kind words make any difference to Rolf's real son?

"The extra money will be a help," added Rolf.

That was the important part. Maybe Erik could fish through the ice in the winter, and there might still be rabbits to snare, but there was so much they had to buy. The flour Rolf had bought today would last just a few weeks, and the potatoes Erik had bought would be gone even sooner. They would soon need kerosene for the lamps. Elsa had grown out of her shoes and Erik's pinched his toes.

"I can work," Erik said.

"Just while they're in this area. When they move on, I might go with them, but you'll stay here and take care of your ma and the livestock."

That night Erik spread his straw-filled ticking on the floor near the stove as he had since the nights had grown cold. Long before dawn, he woke to see Rolf building a fire. They rolled their blankets with a clean shirt or two and tied the bundles with string. Inga made them porridge and Elsa bounced out of bed to pour tea.

"Will they feed you where you work? Should I get some flatbread?"

Erik glanced at Rolf, but his mother answered. "Kirsten told me the crew has a cook for the threshers. They'll eat better than us."

Erik thought Elsa looked disappointed.

"You'll have work to do while we're gone," said Rolf, setting down his cup. "You'll need to lock Tess in the barn at night, so your ma can milk in the morning. Tie her up tight. If she's loose in the barn, she'll trample the feed Erik gathered."

"And eat it," Erik added.

"I can do that," said Elsa.

"And," Rolf went on, "tie a rope to the handle of the washtub and drag it across the prairie. Fill that tub a couple times every day with buffalo chips or dry cow chips and anything else that will burn. We're going to need a lot of fuel for the winter."

Elsa's face fell.

"It won't be hard to keep this house warm in the

winter." Inga's voice was comforting. "Not a breath of wind gets through, except a bit around the door and windows."

Well, thought Erik, something good about the sod house. It was dark, full of bugs, and the floor made everything dirty, but at least it kept out the wind.

He and Rolf left a few minutes later, walking. The threshers were working about eight kilometres away, so they moved briskly. Erik's heart quickened as he heard the big steam engine roaring long before they could see it. Just as it came into sight, they heard several short blasts of the whistle.

The sun was only a faint line on the horizon when they walked into the field, but the men were already at work. Some loaded wagons with bundles of grain, others pitched straw into the big steam engine or hauled water.

The foreman met them as they neared the machinery. "Humph," he said. "Thought you weren't coming." He looked at Erik. "Not very big, are you?"

"I'm strong," Erik replied stoutly.

"We'll see how strong you are. Grab a fork and throw sheaves into the separator." The words made little sense to Erik, but he followed the man's hand as he pointed toward one of the wagons.

"Get up there with the man in the green coat. That's Angus. He's fast and he knows how to do it." The man spoke quickly and in heavily accented English. Erik understood about a fork and a man with a green coat named Angus. He cast an anxious look at Rolf. Rolf took Erik's bedroll and nodded encouragingly. Erik walked hesitantly toward the wagon containing the man in the green coat, just as it moved up beside what he took to be the threshing machine.

Erik climbed onto the wagon and pulled the pitchfork from the side of the box.

Angus glanced at Erik. He asked a question and Erik looked at him blankly. The man jammed his fork into a bundle of grain and hoisted it in the air. "Sheaves," he yelled over the noise of the machinery. "Have you ever pitched sheaves before?"

Erik shook his head. Whatever the man had said, he knew the answer was no. Nothing they'd done on his grandfather's farm looked remotely like this. The man shook his head in turn and tossed the load into the wide mouth of the threshing machine.

"Doesn't matter," he said. "Get pitching."

Erik watched him for a few seconds, then tried to lift a sheaf with his own fork. It was heavy and awkward and his first thought was that he wouldn't be able to do it. For all that he'd said he was strong, he was going to fail before he'd worked five minutes.

He glanced quickly toward Angus and saw how he held his fork. Moving his into the same position, Erik tried again. This time he managed to lift the sheaf. Cautiously he stretched out his arms, and with a little toss, fed in the sheaf.

He'd done it! He picked up another and repeated the move. Slowly he found a rhythm, but even as he worked, he knew that Angus was doing three or four times as many.

Never mind, Erik told himself. He was working, and

maybe they would buy a sack of oatmeal and a tin of coffee because he helped.

When the wagon was empty, Angus moved it forward and another quickly took its place. Angus and Erik jumped onto the new wagon and the driver took the empty wagon away. During the short break between pitching sheaves, Erik stretched his aching muscles and glanced around. There were men everywhere, but he didn't see Rolf.

Erik threw the first sheaf into the threshing machine while Angus climbed up and grabbed his fork. They didn't talk; the machine was too loud. Erik grew hot from the work, but didn't take off his coat, knowing how scratchy the straw would be on his arms. Sweat ran down his face and he wondered how long it was till noon.

Dinner was more food than Erik had ever seen in his life. Roast pork and mashed potatoes, turnips and carrots. There were big round loaves of bread, cut into thick slices, and huge pieces of pie. Erik was amazed at how much the men ate.

"Do you work as little as you eat?" one of them asked Erik.

He felt his face turn red. Instead of answering he took another bite of pie, though he was sure there was no room inside for it.

Erik saw Rolf look at him from the far end of the table, but surprisingly it was Angus who answered.

"He works hard," he said, pausing to accept another piece of pie from the cook. "He'll eat more tomorrow."

Erik leaned back against the wall of the wagon and

wondered if he would. The man beside him looked at Erik's pie. "You going to eat that?" he asked in an undertone.

Erik answered with a shake of his head. The man, bearded and thin, reached over and slid the plate on top of his own. "Hate to see it go to waste, good raisin pie like that."

Raisin pie, thought Erik. He'd never tasted it before. It had been good, though. If Angus was right, he'd be able to eat a whole piece tomorrow, or maybe the next day. He leaned back and closed his eyes for just a moment.

The afternoon was just like the morning, only longer, with the wind blowing dirt in Erik's face and chaff in his eyes. When the cook brought out doughnuts and lemonade, he didn't know if he could lift the glass, let alone another sheaf of wheat. After dark, when they stopped for supper, Erik ate less than he had at noon, his only concerns being where were they going to sleep and how soon could he get there.

Just as there was a roofed-in wagon for cooking and eating, there was a wagon for sleeping. Erik and Rolf each found an empty bunk among those built into the sides of the wagon. Erik went to sleep immediately, oblivious to the talk and laughter around him.

The second day was harder than the first. Erik's arms and back ached, but the blisters on his hands were worse. Even eating was painful. When Erik got up from the table at noon, Angus stopped him.

"Wait a bit. We'll see if the cook can help your hands. When Erik left the cook wagon a few minutes later, the palms of his hands were wrapped in strips of cloth. They still hurt, but he knew he could get through the day.

Saturday night, Erik and Rolf starting walking home, but were offered a ride partway. Erik leaned against his bedroll in the back of the wagon, glad the first week had only been four days long.

When they walked into the sod house, Erik knew he was home. It didn't matter that it was a dirt house with dirt walls and a dirt floor. It was warm, and the lamp on the table had a welcoming glow.

His mother sat in her rocking chair close to the light, knitting something white. Elsa bounced up from the bench where she was writing on her slate. She hugged Rolf, and would have hugged Erik, but he stepped sideways. Digging into a pocket in his jacket, he pulled out two one-dollar bills and placed them on the table.

"Two dollars," exclaimed Elsa, impressed.

"It's not so much," said Erik. "Rolf has eight."

"Why don't you have eight?" Elsa exclaimed. "Didn't you work as hard?"

"Erik worked hard," Rolf assured her. "They pay boys less."

"That's not fair," she said.

"One of the men told me that at some places boys only get twenty-five cents a day," said Erik. "I'm happy with this."

"It will buy you winter boots," said his mother, rising slowly from the rocking chair, and coming to hug them both. Erik let her hug him, startled to realize that she was bigger than she used to be, but only in the front.

She was going to have a baby! Erik stared at her, too surprised to say anything.

"What's the matter, Erik?" she asked. "Is the work too hard for you?"

"No, no, of course not," he stammered. He nodded at the money on the table. "I thought you could use if for food."

"You will need boots," she said, "Or you won't be able to work outside."

Erik didn't argue. Taking off his coat, he spread his mattress on the dirt floor near the stove, then covered it with his blankets.

"Are you going to bed now?" asked Elsa, sounding disappointed.

Erik didn't answer. He lay down and closed his eyes and that was the last thing he knew for a long time.

CHAPTER TWELVE

Tapper

Inga was making breakfast when Erik woke up the next morning. He pulled on his boots and reached for his coat.

"I'll eat when I get back from the spring."

His mother smiled. "Rolf's already gone."

"What?" Erik swung around, glancing from the empty bed to the hook where Rolf's coat usually hung. "I didn't hear him leave."

"You were sleeping so soundly, we let you be."

"I'll milk the cow, then."

"I did that." She set a cup of coffee on the table. "Have your breakfast."

"Well," said Erik, after a long pause. "I guess I will!"

When Rolf got back with the water, Erik helped unload the barrels, then they drove into Green Valley for church. The owner of one of the new stores had offered the upstairs whenever the travelling pastor was in the area.

Afterwards the men talked about a school.

"We have to get it built before winter," one declared.

"But everyone is so busy," another protested.

"We have a teacher," someone else pointed out, "and we have students. If we get the school built, we can use it on Sundays till we have a church building."

"All the churches will want to use it."

"Then we'll have to take turns."

"We don't have a pastor most of the time anyway."

Erik was glad there was a Norwegian church for them to attend, even if it was only occasionally. He struggled with English enough; at least he didn't have to do it at church. His mother, at home most of the time, still knew little English.

Erik and Elsa walked to Lars and Kirsten's afterwards, arriving before Rolf and Inga with the oxen.

"Could you call Olaf?" Kirsten asked Erik as she tied her apron. "I'll get the food on the table. I expect you'll find him with the horses."

Hearing sounds behind the stable, Erik found Olaf pouring a stream of water over the back of a dark bay horse.

The horse shivered and moved restlessly.

"You giving that horse a bath?" Erik asked.

"Oh, it's you," Olaf said, setting the pail on the ground. "Come and take a look."

There was something wrong with the horse. Erik stepped up beside Olaf, staring at the animal. Its back was ripped in long, jagged strips from its neck to the Bar C brand on its hip, the flesh showing red and raw.

"What happened?" Erik asked, horrified. "How did he get those gashes?"

"Some kind of cat. Bobcat, cougar. No one knows for sure." Olaf wiped some of the water away from the horse's sides, careful not to touch its injuries. "See those bite marks on his neck?"

Erik came closer. "It's a wonder he's still alive!"

"Pete was going to shoot him. I asked if I could try to help him. He said, 'If that crowbait can walk, you can have him, he's no good to me.' He walked, so I brought him here. Folks tell me he won't heal unless I can keep the wounds clean, so that's what I'm doing. He doesn't like this one bit, but he stands like he knows it'll help."

Olaf grabbed a handful of oats from a pail and offered it to the horse. "Here, Tapper, have a treat for being such a brave fellow." The horse lipped up the grain from his flat palm, then looked around for more. Olaf laughed softly and untied the lead rope.

"What did you call him?" asked Erik, following them into the stable.

"Tapper."

"Tapper," repeated Erik. It was the Norwegian word for brave. "It's a good name for him. He'll need to be brave to recover from this."

Tapper didn't look brave now. His head hung down and his brown coat was dull.

"How long have you had him?"

"Just a few days, not even a week. He's already looking better." Olaf led the horse into a stall and forked in some hay.

Looking at Tapper now, Erik didn't want to see him a week ago.

Elsa poked her head into the stable. "There you are!"

she announced triumphantly. "Erik, you were supposed to bring Olaf in for dinner."

"Sorry. I forgot."

Elsa stared, horrified, at Tapper. "Oh, the poor horse," she exclaimed, her eyes shiny with tears.

"Looks a mess, doesn't he?" said Olaf. He smiled and touched her shoulder. "Don't worry. He's already getting better."

Tapper took a mouthful of hay and looked back over his shoulder at them.

"See," said Erik. "He's fine."

"Did you say dinner?" Olaf asked.

Erik took Elsa's arm and led her out of the stable. "Come on. Let's go eat."

Kirsten had made a big pot of stew and vegetables. Erik was hungry and filled his plate twice. He was still working on his second helping when Olaf stood up.

"Going out?" Lars asked.

"*Ja,* I'm meeting a friend."

"Can't that wait?" asked Kirsten. "We have guests."

Olaf's eyes flicked quickly to Rolf and away again.

"I made plans," he said. "They're expecting me."

He grabbed his coat from a hook near the door and was gone. Lars opened his mouth to say something, then looked at Kirsten and closed it again.

"How is threshing?" Kirsten asked Erik. "I hear it's hard work."

Erik told her about his days with the crew. The conversation turned to the new people in Green Valley, but Erik's thoughts stayed with Olaf. He was relieved when he was able to go outside.

He glanced up and down the street, but saw no sign of Olaf. Inside the stable, he found Elsa talking to Tapper.

"I brought him a carrot," she said. "He liked it."

Erik eyes flicked to Tapper's back, then quickly away.

"It makes me feel sick," Elsa said softly, "but if you look real close you can see where it's starting to heal."

Erik didn't want to look close. Instead he moved around the stable, talking to the buggy horses, Molly and Star, and the two big horses Olaf used with Gunnar Haugen's team for hauling lumber.

"Want to go for a walk?" Elsa asked. "I want to see the whole town."

"I guess so."

It had warmed up quite a bit since morning, but to Erik, something in the air said winter was coming.

A few men were building, but most had taken Sunday off. Other people were walking around like Erik and Elsa, seeing the town that had sprung up so quickly.

North of the buildings, children played near three or four large white tents. Erik saw the boy he'd met earlier in the week, talking to a younger boy.

"Colin," Erik called, heading in his direction.

Colin saw him, a big smile crossing his face.

"I thought you were moving to a farm," Erik said after they'd greeted each other and introduced Elsa.

"We were going to homestead, but there's no free land close by," Colin said. "Da's talking about moving further west."

"That's too bad," said Erik.

"Why did you come here," asked Elsa, "if there's no land?"

"There were advertisements in the newspapers in Ontario," said Colin, "talking about Green Valley, the next boom town. It sounded like a good place to live."

They walked together down the street as they talked. Erik and Elsa stumbled over their English, but also found Colin's Irish accent a challenge.

A couple of blocks away, the livery stable was taking shape. Erik saw the cowboy, Jim, on a ladder, holding a roof beam in place as Olaf swung a hammer.

"You watch yourself in those fancy boots," they heard Olaf say. "You could fall."

"You should get a pair of these," Jim retorted, "instead of those sodbuster boots of yours. Can't ride a horse in anything that looks like that."

"*Hallo,* Olaf!" called Elsa.

Olaf's head jerked. At first Erik thought he was angry, but then he smiled at Elsa, calling out a greeting.

"Come on," said Erik. "Let's go." He stepped away quickly, hoping Olaf wouldn't think they'd followed him.

"Why the hurry?" asked Colin as he and Elsa caught up with Erik.

"He's not supposed to work on Sunday, is he?" Elsa asked at the same moment.

"I don't think he cares," said Erik.

"Do you know those men?" asked Colin.

"Olaf is our brother," said Elsa proudly.

At the same moment Erik said, "*Ja,* he's our cousin."

Colin looked from one to the other. "Your cousin,

your brother?" he repeated. "Which is he?"

Elsa giggled. "Both," she said, then tried to explain to Colin.

"I saw the other one before," Colin said. "With a man called Pete. He wanted my father to go to North Dakota to get horses. Da said no. He thought Pete was crooked."

"Crooked?" said Erik. "What do you mean?"

"Dishonest. Lying."

"Ohhh," breathed Elsa.

By now they'd left the buildings behind and reached the site of the railway terminus. "My father is working here instead," Colin said. "He doesn't make as much money, but he knows it's legal."

Track was laid out in a huge triangle, with a length of straight track going beyond each point.

"This is the wye," explained Colin. "Da showed me how it works. They aren't going to build a bridge over the river for years, so the trains from Moose Jaw have to turn around here.

"The train drives onto that arm of the triangle." Colin pointed to the wye as he spoke. "Then it backs down the second arm. When the engine reaches the join between the second and third arm, the train drives forward again, going back the way it came."

"That's amazing," said Erik. He stepped onto the track, balancing on the rail. "One day we'll ship grain on these tracks."

He jumped down, following Colin and Elsa back into town. Colin taught Elsa some new words in English and

Elsa repeated them, Irish accent and all. Erik barely listened. His mind was already back with Olaf, wondering about his friends.

A thick layer of frost covered the ground the next morning when Rolf and Erik walked back to the threshing crew. Erik pitched sheaves two more weeks, bringing six dollars home to his mother. The blisters on his hands healed, and after the first week his arms hardly ached and he could eat as much as most of the men. Often he had two pieces of pie. He liked them all, but pumpkin and lemon were his favourites.

When the threshers moved out of the area, instead of going with them, Rolf got work alongside Colin's father building the train track going southeast. Eventually the crew from Green Valley would meet the tracks being built northwest from Moose Jaw, and Rolf would be out of another job.

Erik still hauled water for the house and the animals, breaking through ice at the spring. There was less water there each time, and he worried it would stop flowing altogether. Once it snowed, the animals could eat it and they'd melt some for the house.

Whenever he was in town, Erik stepped into the stable behind the lumberyard to see Tapper. Sometimes Olaf was there, talking to Tapper, pouring water over the deeper injuries that hadn't yet healed. Tapper's coat looked better and his eyes were bright when he turned to welcome Erik. Olaf looked different, too, dressed in cowboy clothes, a package of tobacco stuffed in his vest pocket.

Most of the time Olaf was away, so Erik carried water from the town well to pour over Tapper's back. When the horse shivered, he spoke to him softly, promising he would be healed by spring.

Rolf finished working for the railroad one day in late November when the track his crew was building met the track from Moose Jaw. A couple of days later, Erik and Colin cheered with the rest of the town as the first train steamed into Green Valley. Erik waded through the newly fallen snow, loading wooden crates onto Lars's wagon, wearing new boots bought with money from pitching sheaves.

Rolf found work building houses, so Erik still had to do the outside work at home. Inga rested more, leaving Elsa to cook and clean. Erik helped Elsa churn butter, too, which Rolf took to town to trade at the store for groceries.

One Monday at the beginning of December, Rolf joined two other men on the train to Moose Jaw, looking for a pastor for the Norwegian church. Tuesday, Erik thought his mother looked unwell, and on Wednesday she didn't get out of bed. His heart plunged when he came in from feeding the livestock and saw her fevered face.

"The wind is blowing hard," he said, shaking snow from his coat.

"Mama's worse," said Elsa. "She hasn't woken since you went outside. I can barely hear her breathe." She snuggled beside Inga, her own face flushed.

Erik crouched by the bed. He touched his mother's forehead, feeling the heat against his cold hand. Her eyes fluttered open.

"What do you want us to do? How can we help you?"

"Rolf." The word was a whisper.

"He's not here," Erik said. "He's gone to Moose Jaw, remember? He'll be back in a day or two."

His mother didn't answer. She hugged the blanket closer, her eyes drifting shut.

Erik took his own blanket out of the chest, spreading it over her.

Elsa looked up, her eyes pleading for him to do something. "She needs a doctor. I know she does."

Erik looked out the window, seeing nothing but blackness, thinking of his mother and the unborn baby.

The wind whistled mournfully through the cracks around the windows and Erik nodded his head. He had to do something. There was no one else.

CHAPTER THIRTEEN

Blizzard

"Uncle Lars has a sleigh," said Erik. "He can bring Aunt Kirsten."

"A doctor," said Elsa. "Mama needs the doctor."

Erik layered on a second pair of trousers, then added his heavy sweater. His mother had knitted that sweater for him two years before, in her rocking chair beside Grandfather's fireplace. It had been too big for him then, but now it fit just right.

He tugged on his coat and hat, wrapped a scarf around his head, and shoved his feet into his boots.

"Keep the fire going," he said. "I'll bring in more fuel. Don't let it go out."

Elsa nodded. The chips burned quickly, but kept the room warm. Erik went outside and quickly filled a sack. He dumped it into the box, then headed back outside.

Snow swirled around him as he hurried back to the house. He slammed the door shut, glancing at his mother. She hadn't moved. Erik dropped the sack near the stove and pulled his skis out from behind the bed.

Elsa watched silently, her eyes wide. "Are you going to ski to town?"

"It'll be faster than the oxen, even if I could find them in the dark."

"I'm scared," said Elsa, so quietly Erik could barely hear her. She crawled under the blankets with her mother.

"You'll be fine. You don't have to go outside for anything, but you must keep the fire burning." Erik put on his mitts, grabbed the wooden ski poles and opened the door. "Latch the door behind me," he said, and stepped out into the wind and the snow.

Erik knew he couldn't set off across the prairie. He'd be lost in minutes. He had to follow the trail.

It felt good to have the skis on his feet again, to get into the rhythm. Left, right, left, right. He crossed their own land quickly, then turned right, skiing beside the trail where the snow was smoother. The trail had drifted in a bit, but he could still tell where it was.

The wind blew straight out of the west into Erik's face. He stopped to rearrange his scarf, leaving only his eyes uncovered. His breath dampened the scarf immediately, then it froze against his face.

A dark shadow crossed the trail ahead. A coyote? A wolf? Erik's heart thumped harder as the shadow became one with the darkness.

One, two, three, four. He found himself counting each time he shoved a pole into the snow and forced himself to think of something else. His mother, lying unaware on the bed. He hoped Elsa didn't fall asleep and forget to feed the fire.

The wind cut through his clothes and froze his eyelashes. Trying not to think about the cold, he started counting his strides again.

He forced himself to think of Olaf. He hadn't heard what Olaf was doing since the train started coming to Green Valley. Maybe he was building, like Rolf.

Erik stopped and rewound his scarf, putting the frozen part at the back. He tugged his cap down low over his forehead and set off again. He could still see the shadow of the trail on his left side, so he knew he was safe.

Left, right, left, right.

It was early evening, just past six o'clock, but dark as midnight. Not that he should complain about the dark. Winter days in Norway were even shorter than here, though these were short enough, compared with summer.

Summer in Norway, now. He had never wanted to go to bed; it had seemed wrong to sleep when it was still bright outside. His mother just darkened the room and told him there would be more sunshine the next day.

Trying not to think about whether she would see more sunshine, Erik found himself counting again. He shook his head and thought about the turn ahead. If he missed it, he would bypass the town completely and hit the river hills. Then he'd have to turn around and head southeast.

Unless he lost the trail and changed direction without realizing it. He peered through the darkness at his side, straining to see the shadow of the wheel ruts.

The wind whipped the falling snow into a swirling darkness, hiding everything. Hiding the trail.

Fear clutched Erik's heart. Turning slightly to the left, he moved slowly, with shorter strides. The trail had to be here. He'd been watching it all along.

His left ski hit a dip, then the right ski. He bent and touched the ground. Relief ran through him. "Thank you, God," he whispered. He must be close to the turnoff. He stepped carefully across the trail, then, skiing parallel to the tracks, lengthened his stride.

Left, right, left, right.

Maybe three kilometres more, he told himself. And he could ski fast. All those times he and his friend Andreas had skied together, they'd never skied slowly. Always they'd competed to see who was faster. It was usually Andreas because he was taller and had longer skis. Erik had won sometimes, and would more easily now.

Andreas hadn't built a sod house or pitched sheaves.

Erik had no trouble recognizing the turnoff when his skis hit the ruts. He stopped to rearrange his scarf once more, then stepped over the cross trail and turned south. Only a kilometre to go, he told himself, and slid into the rhythm again.

Left, right, left, right.

He was skiing sideways to the wind now, working hard to stay upright, straining to see in the darkness.

The snow fought against his skis. Every glide took so much effort, he didn't know how much longer he could keep skiing. And cold, he'd never been so cold. Maybe if he stopped to rest…just for a minute.

He shouldn't be out in this blizzard anyway. When the weather was better he'd go on again.

After his rest.

CHAPTER FOURTEEN

Warmth

An image of his mother filled Erik's mind. In bed in the sod house, sick and needing help. He couldn't rest now.

He leaned forward, reaching out with his poles.

Left, right, left, right.

He was watching for the trail into town. If he missed it, he would really be lost. He could ski all the way to – he stopped the thought. He didn't know where, but he could go a long way.

He was counting his glides again. It irritated him, and he tried to think of something else. Rolf. His stepfather. The only father Elsa had known.

Erik pictured their real father coming home from the ocean, smelling of fish and the sea, swinging Erik into the air. Was it a memory, or had he made it up from stories his mother told? He didn't know.

His skis hit a ridge. Erik jerked and started to fall. Jamming his poles into the snow, he righted himself. He'd found the trail into town.

Forgetting he was tired, he swung his skis around and pushed forward. Minutes later, he glimpsed lights flickering through the swirling snow. He had no idea which house held the doctor, but he could find the lumberyard.

He banged on Lars and Kirsten's door, then knelt to unfasten his skis.

"Erik!" Lars opened the door wide. "How did you get here? What's wrong?"

"It's Ma." Erik picked up his skis and stepped inside. "She's sick. Elsa thinks she needs a doctor."

"Is it the baby?" Kirsten whisked Erik to a chair by the stove, pulling off his frozen coat and scarf. In a moment he was wrapped in a blanket, a cup of milky tea warming his hands. He told them what he knew, only vaguely aware of activity around him.

He sipped half the tea, then set the cup on the floor. Leaning back in the chair, his eyes closed.

A hand on his shoulder wakened him.

"We're going now," Kirsten said. "You can sleep on Olaf's bed."

"I'll come with you," said Erik. He jumped to his feet, letting the blanket fall to the bare wooden floor.

"No, no." Kirsten, picked up the blanket and draped it around his shoulders. "You've done enough. The doctor is out with Lars, harnessing the horses. I'll stay with your mama, and Lars can bring you home tomorrow." She put her hand on Erik's back and gently turned him toward a narrow bed in the corner. "Go to sleep now."

The next thing Erik knew, someone was stoking the fire. The room was dark, but he dimly saw Olaf when he lifted a lid on the stove.

He must have made a sound, for Olaf turned and looked at him.

"Erik," he said, surprised. "What are you doing here?"

"My mother is sick," said Erik. "Uncle Lars and Aunt Kirsten took the doctor to her."

"My fa –" began Olaf. "Rolf, I mean, he isn't there?"

"No, he's gone to Moose Jaw." When Olaf still looked at him, Erik added, "To look for a pastor."

"Oh, I see." In the faint light from the fire Olaf went to the table and lit the kerosene lamp. It took him several tries. His hands must be too cold to work properly, thought Erik, feeling more awake. He watched Olaf adjust the wick.

"Where were you tonight?" Erik pushed himself up on the bed. The wall was cold against his back, so he shoved a pillow behind him.

"With friends."

Olaf picked up a round tin box from the table. He pulled out a cookie and took a bite, then brought the tin over to Erik. Erik took a ginger cookie, wishing it were something more filling. He remembered he and Elsa hadn't had supper. He ate the cookie in three bites, and looked up to see Olaf holding the tin out again. Erik took several more.

Olaf put the tin back on the table and dropped into a rocking chair.

Erik could smell horses on Olaf, but he could smell alcohol, too. "Where were you?" he blurted out, then realized he'd already asked that question.

"At Pete's livery stable," said Olaf, surprising Erik with a different answer.

Erik paused in mid-chew.

"This late at night?"

"Sure, why not?" Olaf settled back into the rocking chair. "Some of the men meet there to play cards and talk."

"Isn't it cold?"

"We're not with the horses," said Olaf, sounding disgusted. "We sit in the back room where Pete lives."

Erik ate another cookie, remembering that Colin's father had called Pete crooked. His thoughts were interrupted by a snore. Olaf had fallen asleep in the chair, a half-eaten cookie in his hand. Erik draped a blanket over Olaf, blew out the lamp, and crawled into the bed.

When he woke again it was daylight, and the room was icy cold. Erik made up the fire in the stove, trying not to disturb Olaf, who'd moved onto the bed in the other room.

Snow fell into the house when Erik opened the door. He couldn't see any footprints, not even Olaf's.

There was nothing he could do now, not till it stopped snowing or Lars came back. He looked around for something to eat, finding flatbread. After feeding the fire again, he wrapped himself in a blanket on the bed and dozed off.

The next time he woke, Erik scraped frost from a window and saw it had stopped blowing. He pulled on his warm clothes and walked down the street, amazed to see drifts a metre or more tall on the west sides of buildings, while in sheltered places the snow barely covered the ground. Back at the house, he looked for a shovel, finally taking one from the store. He was clearing in front of the building when he saw Lars's sleigh.

"How's my mother? What did the doctor say?"

Lars stopped the sleigh. "She has influenza. Kirsten stayed to nurse her, but we don't think you should go back right now. The house is too small, and there's no reason to risk your getting sick as well."

"But Elsa –" began Erik.

"Elsa may already have the influenza," said Lars. "She had a fever when we arrived. The doctor left medicine for both of them and will check on them tomorrow." Lars looked at Erik from under his thick eyebrows. "How do you feel?"

"I'm fine," said Erik impatiently.

"Good. The doctor thinks your mother should be fine, too, in a few days."

Erik opened his mouth to speak, but Lars snapped the reins and the sleigh moved around the corner of the building.

Following the sleigh, Erik found it stopped by a drift blocking the stable door.

Lars left the horses standing, and went into the store, reappearing a moment later with another shovel.

"My shovel is locked in the stable behind that drift!" Lars plunged the shovel into the packed snow.

Erik tossed a scoopful of snow toward the piles of lumber. "I have to go home," he said. "If I'm not there, who will milk the cow and bring in snow to melt for water?"

"Kirsten can do those things."

"I'll ski out," said Erik.

"Last night it looked like skiing was too difficult for you."

"Last night was dark and stormy," said Erik. "Today is different."

"They should be fine without you today."

"There will be snow to shovel," said Erik, tossing another heavy scoopful.

"Not so much as here. The shed door faces east so the snow didn't block it. I had no trouble getting the horses out this morning."

"I'll go anyway," said Erik. "When we finish digging out the stable."

"When we're done this," said Lars. "We'll have something to eat, then we'll see."

Once they'd cleared the door to the stable, Erik headed straight for Tapper's stall. He stroked his neck, offering him a handful of oats before helping Lars feed and water all five horses.

In the house, Olaf fried bacon. Lars tried once more to persuade Erik to stay, then let him go with a warning not to get stuck in the snow.

Erik grinned. "That's what skis are for," he said. "To keep me on top of the snow."

The ruts he'd followed the night before had turned into short, lumpy drifts. Beside the trail, the grass was filled with packed snow. Erik skied easily over the smooth places, only slowing down where a protrusion had attracted more snow.

The doctor says she'll be fine. The words repeated themselves over in Erik's head as he crossed kilometres of dazzling snow. *The doctor says she'll be fine.*

CHAPTER FIFTEEN

Shovelling

The snow had drifted in around the buildings in the yard, carving oddly shaped snow sculptures. The chicken hutch was completely buried under the largest drift.

Erik hurriedly stepped out of his skis and, grabbing the shovel from the shed, started digging. When he reached the door of the hutch, a hen stuck out her head and pecked at his shovel.

"So you haven't smothered!" exclaimed Erik. He cautiously dug out the snow that had drifted into the hutch, then fetched grain from the shed.

Inside the house, he stamped the snow off his boots, waiting for his eyes to adjust.

"Erik!" Kirsten's voice came to him from somewhere near the stove. "You didn't need to come out. I already milked the cow."

"*Takk,*" he said. "But there's snow to shovel."

"True." He saw her now, stirring a kettle on the stove. "Would you like some potato soup?"

"Thank you." Erik stepped out of his boots and approached the bed. His mother was asleep, but Elsa's eyes were open, watching him.

"So what are you doing lying around?" he asked, hiding his worry by teasing. "You were supposed to take care of Ma."

"It's warm under the blankets," she told him.

"You should shovel snow," said Erik. "That will warm you up, too."

"Is there much snow?" asked Elsa.

"*Ja,*" said Erik. "Too much." He slid into the bench at the table and picked up his spoon.

"Ma still looks sick," he said, his voice low.

"The doctor says it'll take a while, but she should recover," said Kirsten. "He's not worried about Elsa. He's coming back tomorrow to check on them."

Erik shovelled paths from the house to the out-house and the shed. While he worked, he wondered about the oxen. He had no idea where they were, or if they'd find enough grass to eat. They hadn't strayed far in the past, but he didn't know what they'd do now there was more snow.

Men on the threshing crew had told stories of the winter of 06–07 when the grass was buried under deep snow and thousands of cattle died of starvation. The snow wasn't that deep now, but more could come any day.

Erik shovelled a clearing by the shed, planning a corral in his mind. It should have wooden rails, he thought, but all they had was barbed wire and the posts Olaf had erected in the summer. He was stretching one strand of wire the next day when the doctor drove into the yard.

While he was in the house, Erik made friends with the pinto horse harnessed to the small sleigh.

"What do you think?" Erik asked the moment the doctor stepped outside. "Is she getting better?"

"Of course she's getting better." The doctor climbed into his sleigh and picked up the reins. "She will need to conserve her strength, but she will certainly get better."

Erik watched them drive away, the pinto's hooves barely breaking the surface of the hard-packed snow. Then he turned back to his corral. Awkwardly, with mittened hands, he fastened three strands of barbed wire to the fence posts.

The next morning Erik made a barbed-wire gate and put the cow and calf inside the corral, just for the day. He threw some hay onto the snow and closed the gate while they nosed around in it.

Tomorrow he would have to look for the oxen, but today he would clean the shed.

Afterwards, Erik scooped a pail of clean snow and carried it in to melt. Elsa was sitting up in bed, reading aloud. Her mother lay beside her, eyes closed.

"How are the patients?" he asked.

"I'm almost better," she said, "but Mama's still sick."

"I'm getting better, too," Inga said, her eyes fluttering open. "Kirsten is taking good care of us. What are you doing outside, Erik? You must be frozen."

"Oh, it's not so cold if I keep moving." He slipped off his coat and sat on the edge of the bed, wishing Rolf was there, wishing his mother was as well as she said she was.

When Erik went outside in the morning, the oxen were nosing around in the snow of the corral, eating bits of hay. They'd found their way in through the gate he'd left open after putting Tess and the calf in the shed. Erik couldn't stop smiling as he closed the gate, then brought out an armful of hay for each of them.

It snowed lightly while Erik did the morning chores. When he went back to the house with the milk, Kirsten was cooling Inga's face with a damp cloth.

"Is she worse?" Erik asked, taking a step closer.

"No, no, it's just a bit of a fever."

Erik took off his outdoor clothing, then pulled a chair up by his mother. He stayed there till Kirsten called him for lunch.

They had just finished their smoked fish and rye bread when they heard noises out in the yard. From the door, Erik saw Lars drive his sleigh into the yard, Rolf on the seat beside him.

Stepping into his boots and grabbing his coat, Erik ran out to greet them.

"How is Inga?" Rolf called. He jumped down from the sleigh before Lars had pulled to a stop. Not waiting for an answer, he rushed past Erik into the house.

"She's about the same," Erik told Lars. "Though Aunt Kirsten says she's better."

"Then she must be better," said Lars.

Although Kirsten offered to stay longer, Rolf insisted she go home with Lars. "Erik and I can care for Inga and Elsa," he said.

They hoped fresh meat would help the invalids gain strength. Erik dug a snare out of the snow and reset it. Afterwards, he carried the pickaxe to the river where he'd chipped a hole through the thick ice. By the time the hole was big enough, it was getting dark and he headed home. The hole would be there for him to fish tomorrow.

Within a few days it was as if Elsa had never been ill, but Inga recovered more slowly. She spent a little more time each day sitting in her rocking chair. In the week before Christmas, moving slowly and sitting down often, she taught Elsa how to make Christmas cookies.

In Norway, Christmas was three weeks of visiting and good food. Erik wasn't surprised when the celebrations were much simpler in Canada. The hens laid only the occasional egg now, but Inga had saved several for Christmas baking. She and Elsa made three kinds of cookies, using cardamom and almonds she'd brought from Norway in the bottom of one of her trunks.

Erik stood beside Elsa as she heated the cast-iron *krumkake* maker on the stove, then dropped the first spoonful of batter onto the bottom half. Closing the iron, she pressed the batter between the two halves. After cooking the first side about thirty seconds, she flipped the iron to cook the other side. Without giving it time to cool, Elsa removed the thin, lightly browned circle and shaped it around a wooden cone.

"Look, it's broken," Erik said as Elsa set the first crisp, cone-shaped cookie on a plate.

"No it's not," she exclaimed, then squealed as Erik

broke off a piece, causing the whole cookie to shatter.

"Now I have to eat it," he said, picking up the plate.

"Don't tease your sister," said Inga. She leaned heavily on the table, watching Elsa bake the next cookie.

Other days, Inga and Elsa made wreath-shaped *Berliner kranser* sprinkled with sugar, and deep-fried, cardamom-flavoured *fattigmand.*

On Christmas Eve, Erik took hay from the shrinking pile, feeding all the animals a bit extra, just as his grandfather had taught him. He filled a pail with oats for the chickens, noticing that one of the sacks was almost empty.

Last thing, he grabbed a scant handful of the grain, tossing it on the snow near the slough. In Norway, his grandfather would be feeding the wild birds specially saved stalks of unthreshed grain. Next year, Erik would do that, too.

There was no candle-lit tree waiting behind a closed door, but Elsa and Inga had arranged dried plants in a jar on the table and covered the open shelves with embroidered cloths. Beside Erik's and Elsa's plates were small brown-wrapped parcels. Erik tried to act as if he hadn't noticed them as they ate their Christmas Eve supper of rice porridge, fish balls, and *lefsa.*

"Now we have to sing," declared Elsa, jumping to her feet and stretching out her arms. "Just like we did in Norway."

"We can't," said Erik, "we don't have a tree to circle."

"We can pretend," said Elsa, "that our lamp is a tree."

Rolf and Inga both rose to their feet. Inga and Elsa

each stretched out a hand to Erik.

"Stand up," Rolf said, looking straight at Erik, "and we will circle around the table, like your sister wants."

Erik looked away from Rolf. He wished he was back in Norway, holding his grandfather's big, rough hand, circling the tree the way they had done for as long as he could remember. Suddenly he missed Norway worse than ever. Missed his friends, missed family, missed life as he'd known it.

"Erik?" His mother's voice was soft, questioning.

"Hurry up, Erik." Elsa's voice was insistent. "Let's sing *Jeg er sä glad hver Julekveld* just like we always have."

Erik hardly heard them, his attention caught by Rolf's face. He looked sad but encouraging at the same time. "Together," said Rolf. "We'll do it together."

Erik stood. Slowly he reached his hands out to his mother and his sister. He moved with the others while they sang, "I am so glad each Christmas Eve, the night of Jesus' birth," but he couldn't make himself sing.

When they opened their packages, Erik found a folding pocket knife with two blades.

"You can use it to skin rabbits," suggested Elsa, admiring her own brush and mirror set.

"Takk, manga takk," Erik stuttered, knowing they didn't have money to spend on gifts. "But…"

"It's a good knife," said his mother. "Rolf bought it in Moose Jaw."

"It's a small gift," said Rolf, looking embarrassed, "compared to all you've done."

Erik dropped his eyes to the knife, pulling out the

blades and testing their sharpness. He was so happy he didn't know what to say. After a moment he looked up and smiled.

"Together," he said. "We did it together."

The next day they drove the oxen into Green Valley for church and dinner at Lars and Kirsten's.

Erik was excited to see *gjetost* served with the other special foods. "How did you make it?" he asked. "We haven't had any since summer."

"You'll have to get a goat," said Lars. "We bought this at the general store. They had it shipped up from Minnesota."

Erik caught Elsa's eye and they both smiled. Imagine *buying* cheese! Inga and Elsa made cheese, but they couldn't make *gjetost* from cow's milk.

When they'd eaten all the potato dumplings, beef, and mashed rutabagas, Kirsten set the cookies on the table. Seven kinds, just like his mother and grandmother had always made in Norway. While Kirsten refilled their coffee cups, Lars brought out a metal bowl filled with oranges. Erik took an orange, but slipped it into his pocket for later.

When Olaf finished his orange, Erik followed him outside. Tapper nickered as they walked into the stable.

"He's completely healed," Erik exclaimed, seeing the layer of thin skin over the gashes.

"Just one open spot on his shoulder," said Olaf. He ran his hand over Tapper's back. The horse quivered but didn't move. "But he's not ready for a saddle yet, not quite."

On New Year's Day, Kirsten, Lars and Olaf came to the sod house for dinner. Rolf invited Mr. Johnson as well, the bachelor who'd lent them his sod-cutting plough.

He complimented them on their house. "Norwegians make the best sod houses," he said. "I lived in Nebraska before moving up here. Some of them there barely lasted a year."

"If we did it well," said Rolf, "it's because you told us how."

Erik nodded agreement. It was good to learn from those who'd come earlier.

There wasn't room for everyone at the table, so Olaf and Erik took their plates of roasted rabbit and potatoes to a blanket-covered trunk.

"Your snares are still working, I see," said Olaf.

"I have to set them far from the house to catch any-thing. I guess I've frightened the rabbits away from here." He took a bite of the meat and chewed thoughtfully. "I still want to learn to shoot a rifle. I see the wild chickens sometimes when I check my snares at the far slough."

After dinner, Kirsten persuaded Inga to lie down.

"You need to take care of yourself," she said. "Elsa and I will do the dishes, while Erik and Olaf bring in some more snow to melt."

They found a spot behind the house where the snow had drifted, then used a pail to heap the washtub.

"Too bad that well isn't finished," said Olaf.

"If it ever is," said Erik.

"What do you mean?"

Erik shrugged. "I just worry that we'll dig and dig and there won't be water." He grabbed the handle of the washtub. "Then I'll be doing this forever."

"That would make me worry too," said Olaf, struggling with the tub as if it was too heavy to lift.

Erik looked up at him, confused. Olaf met his eyes and burst into laughter.

They were both laughing as they set the washtub on the packed dirt floor by the stove.

Back outside, Olaf leaned against one of the fence poles watching the oxen. They had trampled everything in the corral, so they stretched their necks out over the fence to eat the snow. The cow and calf were there, too, along with Molly and Star, Lars's team.

"My grandfather has horses," Erik said. "And goats. I never saw any oxen till we got to Minnesota."

"They must eat a lot," said Olaf.

"Less than horses," said Erik. "That's what everyone says. We never give them oats."

Olaf grunted, pulling his wide-brimmed hat down to shade his eyes from the glare of the sun. "Have you heard about the cattle that died a couple years ago when there was so much snow?"

"*Ja,*" said Erik. "Men on the threshing crew spoke of it."

"Jim was working for a big ranch south of Swift Current," said Olaf. "The Turkey Track. More than half their cattle died. In the spring they found bodies hanging from trees."

The calf, pushed out by the oxen, came to Erik. She was big now, almost as large as Tess. He scratched her head, trying to imagine snow so deep that cows seeking shelter under trees were really far off the ground.

"The men tried to help the cattle, but there wasn't any feed to give them," Olaf went on. "The cattle just roamed, scratching for grass, but it was buried so deep they couldn't find it. By springtime, there were so few cows, most of the cowboys lost their jobs."

"So that's why Jim works for Pete?"

"I guess so."

"This Pete," Erik began. "Colin O'Brien said he might be *crooked.*"

Though they were speaking Norwegian, Erik used the English word to describe Pete.

Olaf threw his hands in the air in an expression of disgust. "What does Colin O'Brien know about it? He's just a kid. A kid like you."

Erik shook his head, but didn't say anything as the older men came out of the house dressed in their heavy coats and hats with the earflaps pulled down.

"This corral," Rolf was saying. "Olaf put in the fence posts and Erik strung the wire and made the gate. I didn't do anything at all."

"So," Lars said, "it's good to have sons."

Rolf nodded, his eyes on Olaf. "It is," he said. "Sons are a good thing."

Olaf, not looking at Rolf, stepped back from the fence and turned away.

Erik watched Rolf's eyes follow Olaf. He'd said *sons*

ADELE DUECK

but he only looked at Olaf. What if he meant Erik too? Would it be wrong to accept Rolf as a father when his real father was gone?

It was hard to understand Olaf. He could have two fathers, but seemed to have chosen to have none. Erik watched him walk over to the chicken hutch as if the hens were more interesting than the men's conversation.

Shrugging, Erik returned to the house to warm his hands over the stove. His mother was sleeping. Kirsten and Elsa were already setting out coffee and cookies for lunch, though it seemed to Erik they'd just finished dinner. He broke off a small piece of a *krumkake* and popped it in his mouth.

Picking up a Norwegian book, he pulled a chair up close to the stove, wishing the book was in English. Turning the pages without reading, he half-listened to Kirsten and Elsa talk, glad they were friends.

A spider dropped from the tarpaper onto his book. Erik squeezed it between his fingers and jumped to his feet in disgust. How long did they have to live in a dirt house? He turned in a quick circle in the middle of the room and sat down again. There was nowhere to go. Nothing was going to change.

"Erik?"

Erik turned to his mother. She was sitting up, the blanket pushed to the side.

"What's troubling you?" she asked, her voice low.

"I'm fine." Erik forced a smile to his face. "I'm fine."

"I hope you don't mind about," she hesitated, "about the baby."

Where would they put a baby in a sod house? "Babies are good," he said at last. "But we should get a real floor in here before it starts to crawl."

His mother reached out a hand. "Did I ever tell you what a fine boy you are?"

Erik took her hand in his. He felt his face flush and found he couldn't speak.

CHAPTER SIXTEEN

Brothers

Rolf and Erik built a wooden wall to divide the sod house into two rooms. Inga hung a curtain made of flour sacks over the opening. The second room had two narrow bunks built one above each other on the new wall. There was no window in the room, but Rolf made a small table for a candle.

"Are you going to sleep in the tent again next summer?" Elsa asked Erik as they lay in their bunks the first night.

"I don't know," said Erik sleepily. "I haven't thought about it."

"I hope you do," said Elsa. "Then I will have this room all to myself."

Erik looked around, seeing only blackness except for a dim glow through the curtain from the lamp in the other room.

He recalled the birds singing before dawn, the sun warming the canvas, flies buzzing in the heat.

"I might sleep outside again. In the summer."

Afew days later, his mother was still in bed when Erik got up. Rolf had the fire going in the stove and was stirring porridge.

"I want you to go to town," he said quietly. "After breakfast. To bring back the midwife."

"Should I take the wagon?"

"No, you can ski." Rolf put Erik's bowl in front of him and passed the pitcher of milk. "Lars said that when the baby came, he would lend us his sleigh."

Erik got up from the table and went over to one of the windows. He had to scrape off a thick layer of frost before he could see the stars.

He went back to the table. "Do you want me to go right away?"

Rolf glanced toward the bed. Erik followed his look. Inga shook her head. "Wait till it's light out," she said. "You've already done one trip in the dark for me. That's enough."

She didn't look sick like when she had influenza. Relieved, Erik nodded and picked up his spoon.

In the daylight, with no wind, the trail was easy to follow. The sun rose higher, and Erik, squinting against the snow, saw Green Valley in the distance.

He headed straight to the store. Lars stood behind the counter, selling coal to a customer. Erik waited impatiently till the man left.

"Rolf sent me to borrow your sleigh," he said. "Ma's going to have her baby."

Lars closed his ledger. "Do you know where the mid-wife lives?"

Erik shook his head. Lars reached back and untied the apron around his waist. "I'll talk to her. Olaf's out back. Tell him to hitch Star and Molly to the sleigh."

Erik found Olaf in the stable, brushing Tapper. Together, they harnessed the team and brought them outside. Minutes later Kirsten came out of the house, covered head to foot in a fur coat and hat.

"I'm going to your mother," she said, climbing into the sleigh. "I'll send Rolf in, too. We don't need men when a baby is born."

"What's this?" asked Lars, joining them. "I told Mrs. Sorenson I'd pick her up in a few minutes."

"I'll get her," said Kirsten. Her eyes rested on Olaf standing in the doorway to the stable, then she smiled at Erik. "Don't worry," she said. "Your mother will be fine, and you will soon have a new brother or sister."

She snapped the reins and pulled out of the yard.

Lars turned toward the store, then glanced back at Erik. "You want to help me unpack the new shipment?"

Erik glanced at Olaf's grim face.

"In a few minutes," he said.

Lars nodded. "I'll work slowly so there's some left to uncrate when you join me."

Erik followed Olaf into the stable. Olaf dropped onto an overturned pail in the corner. Erik crouched on the floor by the door. Picking up a bit of straw, he turned and twisted it in his hand.

The silence between them became too long to bear.

"This baby," Erik said at last. "We will both be its brother."

There was a long pause before Olaf spoke.

"I never knew my mother. She died when I was born."

It was the fear in the back of Erik's mind, the fear he hadn't voiced, even to himself. He breathed a silent prayer for his mother.

"I called Kirsten *Mor*," said Olaf, "even though I knew she and Lars weren't my real parents." He stood up and brushed straw from his trousers. "I've always known my father gave me away."

Erik thought of Rolf's face when he and Olaf met. "He didn't want to."

"Then why did he do it?"

"Maybe he thought he couldn't look after you alone."

Olaf reached a hand out to Tapper. The horse sniffed it, then tossed his head and backed away.

"He still doesn't trust me."

Erik smiled. "He remembers those cold baths."

Olaf talked softly to Tapper in Norwegian, telling him what good times they would have together when his back healed.

Shivering, Erik went into the store. He helped Lars unpack the new stock, then went to see Colin. The O'Briens had moved into a house when it grew too cold for a tent. To Erik the house didn't seem warm either, not as warm as the sod house. There was frost on the walls and air whistled through gaps between the boards.

Colin set aside his copybook when Erik came in.

"My mother used to be a teacher," he said. "She thinks we should be in school." His mother looked up from her sewing and smiled warmly at Erik. Colin's brother, who'd opened the door, invited Erik to sit on the bench beside him.

"I'm learning to print," Patrick said proudly.

"Show me what you know," said Erik. He watched Patrick print his name on a slate, rubbing out letters and rewriting them till they were perfect.

"Da has started work at the general store," said Colin.

"At the store?" repeated Erik. "Just till spring?"

Colin shrugged. "We're not sure. Ma doesn't want to move again."

"There are so many businesses in town now," Colin's mother said. "It will be a good place to live."

There were many new houses, too. Some, like the O'Briens', were built to rent or sell. Others, bigger and sturdier, belonged to businessmen and the doctor. Even Lars and Kirsten talked of building so they wouldn't have to live behind the store.

Visiting Colin helped Erik forget his mother for a while, but not for long. When he went back to the lumberyard, Rolf was there, silently pacing.

"You'll wear a path in the floor," Lars said. "Look, here's Erik. Why don't you play checkers? It will give you something to think about till Kirsten returns."

Lars got out the checkerboard, but it was a new game to Erik and he couldn't concentrate. When a man with a thin pointed face came in, he sat in Erik's seat, defeating Rolf very quickly.

"Your mind is far away," the man said, getting up to make his purchase. "Perhaps we can play again another day."

It grew dark. Lars invited them to a new restaurant down the street. While they pulled on their coats, he said he'd look for Olaf. When he returned from the stable alone, he shook his head. "Olaf used to work all the time, saving up his money. Now he buys those fancy cowboy clothes and I can never find him when I need him."

He tried to make it into a joke, but Erik thought he was worried. Rolf nodded his head in reply. His face wore the same stony look Erik had seen so often on Olaf's.

There were several other men eating in the restaurant. One of them recognized Rolf. "You looking for work?" he asked. "I'm building a house for my family but need some help."

He glanced at Erik. "I could use you, too, if you know how to hammer." Erik sat up straighter and looked at Rolf.

"I'm sorry," said Rolf. "His mother needs Erik at home, but I should be able to start work tomorrow."

Erik sighed. It's true, there was always work to do at home, but they could do with the money he would earn, too.

Kirsten was in the lean-to when they returned. "You have a beautiful son," she said as soon as Rolf stepped into the room.

A boy!

"Inga is doing well. I'll come out tomorrow to see how she is and will bring some fish balls and dumplings."

Rolf turned around and reached for the door handle. Erik picked up his skis.

"Take the sleigh," suggested Lars.

"No, no, Kirsten will need it tomorrow."

"Then bring it back tomorrow morning when you come in," said Lars. "I insist."

Erik and Rolf travelled in silence. Erik watched the trail, shadowy in the starlight, his mind on his mother and his new brother.

Elsa was sitting in the rocking chair holding a white bundle when they burst into the room. Without waiting to take off his outdoor clothes, Rolf rushed over to the bed.

"Inga, you are truly all right?" He perched on the edge of the bed, leaning over to kiss her.

"Of course I'm all right," said Inga. She reached up and brushed snow from his red hair. "You shouldn't have worried."

"How could I not worry?"

Erik pulled off his coat and stepped out of his snowy boots. Glancing from Elsa, with the baby, to his mother and Rolf, he nodded. How could they not worry, knowing what had happened to Olaf's mother?

The baby was smaller than Erik expected. His dark eyes seemed to look right into Erik's face. Hesitantly, Erik reached out his hand and smoothed it over the downy soft hair. "He looks so wrinkly and red."

Rolf came over, reaching for his son. "Let's see this wrinkly, red fellow," he said. As he picked him up, the baby started to cry.

"What's wrong?" exclaimed Erik. "Is he hurt?"

"Probably thinks I'm not doing this right," said Rolf. He cuddled the baby a moment. "Sit down, Erik."

Surprised, Erik sat, and Rolf placed the baby in his arms.

"His name is Leif," Elsa said, bouncing up and down in her excitement. "And I get to be with him all the time."

A couple of times during the night, Erik heard sounds from the other room. Someone moving around, little cries from the baby. He got up when he heard Rolf tend the stove. Baby Leif snuggled with Inga on the bed, both asleep. Rolf left soon after to go to his new job in town, but Erik waited till it was light before going outside.

He took hay to the calf and oxen, then pushed the remainder into a pile in the corner of the shed. There was so little left, though Erik was feeding less than the cattle needed. He milked Tess, getting half of what she'd given in the fall. Erik noted how her ribs showed sharply against her sides. Thinking of the calf she would have in the spring, he decided to stop milking her to conserve her health.

Coming out of the shed, he saw one of Lars's horses tied to a fence post. Inside the house, Elsa urged Olaf into the rocking chair.

"He's a very good baby," Elsa assured him. "He hardly cries at all."

"He cried last night," said Erik.

"He was hungry," said Elsa confidently. "That's the only time he cries."

Olaf looked worried as Elsa placed the baby in his arms. "I might drop it," he protested.

"Nonsense." Inga smiled at Olaf from the bed. "Nothing will happen."

"Let him hold your finger," said Elsa. "He likes that."

Erik made coffee from melted snow water, glancing over his shoulder occasionally. Olaf rocked Leif, talking to him the same way he spoke to Tapper.

Winter was a good time for a new baby. Erik wasn't as busy as the rest of the year. Leif soon recognized his voice, waving chubby fists when he came near. Olaf stopped by often, bringing food from Kirsten. He taught Leif to play peek-a-boo, and brought a rattle he'd bought in town. He seemed to know when Rolf was working, for he never visited when Rolf was there.

CHAPTER SEVENTEEN

Water

In March, the snow melted and school started in the Presbyterian Church. Rolf wanted Erik at home, but a couple of times a week he let Erik and Elsa walk to Green Valley to school. Elsa made friends with Sara, whose father owned the drugstore. Erik and Colin visited Tapper at noon whenever they could. Erik hoped to ride him one day, when he was completely healed.

Erik fed the last of the hay he'd gathered to the cattle, then let them loose on the prairie, hoping they could find something to eat.

Thin as they were, Rolf still caught the oxen each day, hitching them to the plough. They worked the ground broken the year before and then started breaking new land. When the oxen rested, Rolf dug in the well, using a rope ladder to get up and down. He built cribbing out of wood to support the inside of the well and keep the walls from caving in. As the well got deeper, Rolf lowered the cribbing and Erik pounded together new sections to add at the top.

One Saturday, Erik was hammering on the cribbing when Rolf hollered to him to pull up the pail. Erik carried it over to the firebreak and dumped it. The dirt looked dark against the ground. Erik grabbed a handful of the soil.

"Rolf, Rolf!" he yelled. "It's wet!"

"Hallelujah!" Erik heard Rolf's voice from down in the well. A moment later he tugged on the rope, signalling Erik to pull up another load.

Rolf kept on digging, and Erik carried pail after pail to the firebreak, throwing the dirt wide so it didn't pile up.

As he tossed yet another pail of soil, Erik looked at it closely, then bent down and touched it. Dry.

How could it be dry? It should be getting wetter. They should be hitting water.

Erik went back to the well. He should say something to Rolf. Even with the kerosene lamp, it was dim down there. He probably couldn't see what was happening.

"Last one," yelled Rolf. "I'm coming up."

Erik grabbed the rope and pulled up the pail. By the time he'd emptied it, Rolf was stamping the dirt from his boots.

"A good day's work," Rolf said, clapping Erik on the back. "At this rate, the well will be finished in a few days and I can start seeding."

Erik nodded and forced a smile. Maybe he was wrong. He wouldn't say anything. They would know for sure tomorrow – no, Monday. On Monday they would know.

After church the next day, Olaf took Erik to a corral holding several horses on the edge of town. "I put Tapper here sometimes," he said. "Gives him more exercise." Olaf perched on the top rail of the corral, whistling for Tapper.

Erik patted Tapper's sleek neck. "Quite the brave boy,

aren't you?" Tapper shook his head and nuzzled Erik. "Sorry, I didn't bring you any treats."

"You started seeding yet?" asked Olaf.

"Not yet. We've been working on the well."

"Oh? Hit water?"

"Not...not yet," said Erik. "We're down nine, maybe ten metres. It was damp for a while but now it's dry again."

"Digging it all by hand, are you?"

"Well, Rolf is." Erik noticed how Olaf avoided any direct reference to Rolf. "We better get water soon, I don't think he can dig much further by hand, and well drillers cost money."

"Everything costs money," said Olaf. "Come on, we better get going before they eat all the food."

First thing the next morning, they were back at work on the well. Elsa came out to watch. "Is there any water yet?" she yelled down to Rolf.

There was a long pause.

"No." Rolf's voice floated up to them. "Not yet."

Rolf sent up a couple more pails of the hard grey soil, then tied his pick and shovel to the rope.

"Time to quit," he said when he climbed out. His shoulders slumped and his voice was discouraged. "Looks like it's dry."

Erik looked at the slough, not so far away, overflowing from the spring runoff.

"How can there be water there and not here? It doesn't make sense."

Rolf shrugged. "Not much makes sense."

He carried the yoke over to the oxen and hitched them to the plough. Erik laid boards across the well hole, setting rocks on top to hold them in place. It was just as he feared. All that digging and carrying – and no water.

At least the slough was full. Erik carried water from the slough to fill the barrels by the house. When the barrels were full, he fished out a couple of duck feathers, then watered Tess and her heifer.

Rolf helped Mr. Johnson with his seeding in return for borrowing his harrows. He seeded their own land by hand, half to wheat and half to oats. Erik followed behind with Black and Socks pulling the harrows to smooth the soil and cover the seed.

When they were finished, Rolf harrowed for another neighbour, the same man he'd stooked for in the fall.

Erik always found work to do at home. One day he dug holes in the garden as Elsa dropped in pieces of potato. Another day he applied a new coat of whitewash to the inside of the house. He planned to find trees to start a windbreak behind the house, as soon as he had time.

His first two trees had bright green leaves. His biggest fear was that something would eat them. They should build a fence, or get a dog. A dog would keep the coyotes from the chickens and the rabbits from the garden. He just didn't know where to get one.

When the wheat showed above ground, Erik started tethering the cattle again, to keep them from eating the new plants. One afternoon when Erik went to lead Tess to the slough for water, he found a bull calf curled up beside her. Two weeks later, he started locking Tess in the shed at night again. Inga used the first pail of milk to make a big pot of rice porridge.

Early one June morning, Erik hauled water from the slough for his mother to wash clothes. He was carrying a full pail when a wagon heaped with wood and metal and pulled by two heavy black horses drove into the yard. Holding the reins was a man Erik had never seen before. Beside him was Olaf.

Erik set the pail of water down as the wagon stopped near the dry well. The stranger climbed down and looked at the wooden cover.

"You been digging this well?" he asked Erik with a friendly look.

"Not me," said Erik. "I just hauled up the dirt." Amazed, he watched the man pull away the boards covering the well.

"Gone down close to thirty feet, I'd guess," he said. "Nice cribbing." He held out his hand to Erik. "Name's Charlie," he said. "You must be Erik." Startled, Erik shook his hand. Charlie pulled a three-metre length of slender corkscrew metal from his wagon, then lit a tin lantern.

Erik looked at Olaf. "What are you doing? Did Rolf ask you –" But then he stopped. Rolf wouldn't ask Olaf to do anything. He and Olaf didn't talk.

"I didn't want Leif drinking slough water." Olaf looked embarrassed as he carried a coil of rope to the well.

"See now," said Charlie. "We're going to drill this into the dirt at the bottom of the well. If there's water within ten feet, we'll find it. If not, we add another ten foot section and try again."

He tied the rope onto the auger and dropped it slowly down the well, then hooked the lantern onto his overall straps and lowered himself onto Rolf's rope ladder. Erik and Olaf crouched down to watch.

"Do you need me down there?" asked Olaf.

"Too crowded."

Erik longed to ask Olaf what the man would charge and who would pay for it, but all he could think was how wonderful it would be if they found water.

In the light from the lantern, Erik saw Charlie turn the crank, digging his test drill into the floor of the well. After a few minutes, Charlie pulled out the auger, inspected the dirt it had brought up, then twisted it back down. The third time he cranked the drill back into the well, he hollered, "Hey, Olaf. You better lower down another section of the drill."

Erik's heart sank as Olaf pulled up the rope to tie on the second length of metal.

The man at the bottom pulled out the auger and looked at it again.

"Forget that," he called. "We've got it."

Erik met Olaf's eyes. He was surprised to see joy that matched his own. Olaf dropped the rope back down to bring up the test drill.

When Charlie got up, he set the lantern down on the ground and pulled a handful of damp soil out of his pocket. Erik reached out and touched the soil. It felt cold and wet – dripping wet.

"So there's really water down there."

"I 'spect there is," said the man. "That's how the dirt got wet."

"So we have to dig that much more?" Erik looked at the auger. From the dirt showing in the curves of the drill, he was guessing they needed to go at least three more metres.

"We'll let Gertrude and Sam do it," said the man. "They're quick, you just watch."

Behind him, Erik heard the door of the house open. "Erik," said his mother, "I need more water –" She stopped when she saw Olaf and the other man.

"Hallo, Olaf," she said, switching to her stilted English out of courtesy to the stranger. "I not see you."

Olaf coloured faintly and introduced Inga and Charlie. "He's going to find water in your well," he added.

"Water good," she said hesitantly, "but money… not good."

Charlie jerked his head toward Olaf. "It's on his tab," he said. "Now I gotta work if we're gettin' this well dug."

"Don't worry about the cost," Olaf said hurriedly in Norwegian. "I'm taking care of that."

Her face lit up. "Olaf, you are a dear son." She threw her arms around him and leaned her head against his chest. Olaf's arms came up, and for a brief moment he returned her hug.

"It's for Leif," Olaf said.

"And a dear brother." Then, turning to Erik, she

added, "Bring in a few more pails of water, Erik, then you and Elsa can watch them drill."

By the time Erik got back to the well, the tripod had been replaced by an elaborate drilling apparatus. It turned as Charlie's horses walked in a circle around the well. Periodically, Charlie went down the well, sending up pails of dirt. To keep the soil from piling up, Erik and Olaf emptied the pails in the firebreak on the other side of the yard. Elsa got bored after a while, and went to check the progress of the garden before going back to the house, but Erik stayed outside, helping to build the cribbing while the horses turned the drill.

When noon came, Inga invited them in to eat, but Charlie refused. "Gotta get this done," he said, "but thank you."

Inga brought out bread and cheese to eat as they worked, and they kept going all afternoon.

"Good thing the horses can rest while Charlie scoops out the dirt," said Elsa in the early evening.

Erik brought water from the slough to the horses. "They've worked hard today."

"Vanne! Vanne!" Olaf yelled, holding a pail high. "Water! We have water!"

Erik and Elsa ran to Olaf, followed a moment later by Inga from the house, clutching Leif.

"Is it true?" Elsa cried.

"Oh, it's true enough," said Charlie. He crawled out of the well and headed for his horses, his boots leaving wet prints on the ground.

"We'll go a bit further to get out more dirt," he

said, "but you've definitely got yourself a well." He drilled a while longer, then descended into the well to send up pails of mud and water and install the final section of cribbing.

When Charlie came up the last time, a huge grin split his face. "You just let that sit till tomorrow so the dirt settles and the water comes in." He slapped Olaf on the back, then started dismantling his equipment, piling it back on the wagon.

Erik noticed Olaf glancing around as he harnessed the horses to the wagon. Watching his face, Erik knew the exact moment Rolf walked into the yard.

"Good evening," said Rolf, holding his hand out to Charlie. "I'm Rolf Hanson."

"Charlie Briggs," said Charlie. "Looks like you've got a good well here. I could hardly climb out fast enough!"

"Well?" repeated Rolf, mystified. He walked over to the open hole and peered down, though Erik doubted he could see anything without a light at the bottom.

Erik waited for Olaf to say something, but soon saw he wasn't going to.

"Olaf hired Mr. Briggs to dig the well," said Erik. "He went down about three more metres and hit water."

Rolf stared at Olaf.

"Why don't we drop a pail and see what we bring up?" said Charlie. He grabbed the rope they'd used for lowering the auger and Erik handed him a pail. Everyone watched as Charlie lowered the pail, pulling it up a moment later half full of water.

"It's fillin' fast," said Charlie.

ADELE DUECK

Elsa ran to the house for a cup. Charlie filled it and handed it to Rolf.

Rolf accepted the tin cup with a nod. He took a sip and handed it to Inga who'd come out with Elsa. She tasted it, then Erik and Elsa each had a sip.

Elsa squinched up her face. "It tastes dirty," she said.

"It'll settle out," said Charlie. "Just give it time."

"Good water," said Rolf, his voice cracking. "Thank you, Olaf. This is a wonderful gift."

"I did it for Leif," said Olaf. He turned to the wagon, shoving a piece of wood to the side, then putting it back where it had been. He glanced over his shoulder at Rolf, then shifted his glance quickly to Charlie. "Are you ready to go?"

"Sure thing," said Charlie. "Thanks for the food, Mrs. Hanson," he said. "That bread was sure good."

Rolf shook his hand again. "Thank you, many thanks."

He took a step toward Olaf, but Olaf slipped around the side of the wagon and climbed up.

No one spoke till the wagon was out of sight.

"We need something on the top," said Elsa.

"Ja," said Rolf. "A well head."

Erik glanced at Rolf. He looked completely overwhelmed by what had happened. They had a well, and all because of Olaf, the son who wouldn't speak to him!

Erik picked up a board. "I'll cover it for now."

"Wait!" said Inga. "Let's get more water first."

No one moved as Erik brought up another pail of water, their gift from Olaf.

CHAPTER EIGHTEEN

Threat

The next time Erik saw Olaf, he was riding into their yard on Tapper.

"So what do you think of my horse now?" Olaf asked.

"If he can carry someone as heavy as you on his back, he must be healed." Erik stroked Tapper, the dark brown coat warm and shiny beneath his hand. Though he could see some scars, most were hidden under the saddle.

"Do you want to ride him?"

"I sure do," said Erik. "Right now, do you mean?"

Olaf shrugged. "It's as good a time as any." He dismounted and handed Erik the reins.

Putting his left foot in the stirrup and grabbing the saddle horn, Erik pulled himself up and swung his right leg over Tapper's back.

Tapper pranced in a circle, aware that his rider had changed. Erik pulled on the reins to hold him still.

"Take him for a run," Olaf suggested, giving Tapper a smart slap on his hindquarters. "See what the boy can do."

"I don't –" Erik began, but didn't finish as Tapper broke into a gallop. Erik clenched the reins in one hand and grabbed Tapper's mane with the other.

"Slow down," Erik yelled in Norwegian. Tapper, despite his Norwegian name, didn't understand. He ran as if chased by the wildcat that had attacked him.

Erik forced himself to take a breath and straighten slightly. After a moment he even looked around. They had almost reached the slough with the saskatoon berries and he hadn't fallen off yet. Maybe he wouldn't!

He felt the reins in his hand and gave them a tug, pulling slightly to the left. To his relief, Tapper slowly began turning. Erik tugged harder. He felt Tapper slow down as they crossed a field of wheat, centimetres tall and bright green.

By the time they reached Olaf, Tapper was walking, his coat shiny with sweat.

"So what do you think?" asked Olaf. He took the reins from Erik's unresisting hands.

"He likes to run," breathed Erik. He slid down from the saddle, not sure if his legs would hold him. "I'm not used to that!"

"Me, neither," admitted Olaf. He stroked Tapper's neck. "I can't wait to see how fast he can go when he's completely recovered!"

"You think he'll go faster?" asked Erik incredulously.

"I don't know. I'm looking forward to finding out."

Erik picked up the spade he'd been using and leaned on it for support. "You could have warned me!" he said.

Olaf grinned. "I didn't know what he would do, not for sure!"

Erik eyed Olaf skeptically. "You were hoping he'd throw me," he said.

Olaf shook his head unconvincingly.

"Want to come in the house?" asked Erik. "For coffee?" When he saw Olaf hesitate, he added quickly, "You need to try our new water!"

"I guess I do." Olaf put Tapper in the corral and followed Erik into the house.

Elsa was flopped on her stomach on the bed, teaching Leif to clap his hands.

"Olaf!" she exclaimed. "Come see how smart our brother is!"

Olaf crouched beside the bed, extending a finger for Leif to grab. The baby's hair was coming in red, like his father's. And Olaf's.

"He's going to look like you," Inga said, setting aside her handwork and rising. "He has your eyes."

"You think so?" said Olaf, and Erik thought he was pleased.

With more than fifty businesses and dozens of homes in Green Valley, the town decided to celebrate with a Dominion Day picnic.

On the days that Elsa and Erik walked to school, they saw the preparation work in progress. A half-mile racetrack was laid out near the railroad station, with bleachers for five hundred people rising beside it. A baseball diamond was planned for the centre of the racetrack, and the football field would be to the east.

"Will there be enough people to fill those seats?" Elsa asked one day.

"I don't know where they will come from," said Erik. "There aren't five hundred people in the area."

Kirsten had invited the family to a birthday supper for Lars, so Erik and Elsa didn't go home after school. Elsa went to Sara's house and Erik walked with Colin to Pete's livery stable to pay for boarding the O'Briens' horses.

"It would be better if we had a barn of our own to keep them in," Colin confided. "Da is not always sure they feed the horses what they say they do."

"If he thinks Pete is not honest, why does he keep your horses there?" Erik asked.

Colin shrugged. "He charges less than the other livery stable."

Erik nodded. Saving money was something he understood.

Erik looked around curiously. He'd walked by sometimes when the wide front door was open, but this was the first time he'd been inside. The horses faced the wall, their tails flicking at flies. Every stall was filled; some even had two horses. Some of the horses turned their heads and nickered when the boys walked past. Erik walked slowly, admiring the horses, noting the brands on their hindquarters. Most common was the Boxed Q. He guessed it must be Pete's own brand. None had the same brand as Tapper, the Bar C.

At the end of the centre alley, Erik followed Colin through a door into the back room that Olaf had mentioned. Several men played cards at a table. A tall bottle stood on a side table and a couple more on the floor. Money was scattered on the table, more money than Erik had ever seen in one place.

One of the men stood up when the boys walked in. Erik guessed he was Pete. Older than the other men, he had long brown hair and a scar across his face, partly hidden by his beard. He smiled at the boys, but it didn't reach his eyes.

Colin handed him the money his father had given him. Pete counted it carefully and nodded his head at Colin. "That's good for one more week."

"Da said to get a receipt," said Colin quickly.

"A receipt?" repeated Pete. He laughed shortly. "All right, then." He went to a desk against one wall and pulled a paper out of a drawer. He dipped his pen in the ink, then wrote something on the paper. Without waiting for the ink to dry, he handed it to Colin. Colin glanced at the paper and nodded his head.

"Thank you." He turned to the door, holding the paper carefully.

"Good doing business with you."

One of the men at the table looked up from his cards and Erik recognized Olaf's friend Jim. Erik nodded, but Jim looked at him as if they'd never met.

After dropping the receipt at Colin's house, they walked down to the river through the valley of trees. The water in the river was high and moving quickly. They walked along the shoreline, tossing stones into the rushing water, climbing partway up the hill when there was no room to walk between the water and the brush.

Colin scrambled over a fallen tree trunk and started grabbing at short, sturdy plants, pulling himself up a cliff. Erik walked along the fallen trunk as far as he could, then followed Colin. Once at the top they collapsed on the grass and looked out over the river.

"They want to put a ferry there," said Erik, looking south down the river to where the shore was sloped more gradually. "Then people from that side of the river could buy in Uncle's store."

"Sometimes people ford the river," said Colin. "They drive across right through the water."

"Not today," said Erik. "A horse couldn't walk the river today. Or swim, either."

As he spoke, he heard the whinny of a horse. There were no horses to be seen, not in the water or anywhere else, but Erik knew sounds could carry a long way on a day like this without any wind.

The boys walked along the top of the hills, following a valley, until they looked down on the weathered shack and the corral Erik had seen in the fall. Now it held at least twenty horses.

"Nice horses," said Erik. They scrambled down to the bottom of the coulee. There was no sign of people.

"This is strange," said Colin, his voice hushed. "It doesn't look like a farm."

"And what farmer has so many horses?" asked Erik. He wanted to go up to the horses, but something told him that this wasn't a good place to be.

He heard the sound of hooves and, grabbing Colin's arm, pulled him down behind a clump of bushes.

Peeking through the screen of branches, they saw two horses and riders come into the valley from the south.

The men unsaddled their horses and put them in the corral with the others.

The door of the shack opened and a man came out, stretching and yawning.

"So how are things in town?" he asked.

"Hoppin'," replied one of the men. "Pete wants us to get the rest of these branded."

"I thought he was waiting for his pal from Montana to do it."

"Not any more." The three men leaned against the top rail of the corral. Their voices carried easily to where Erik and Colin were hiding.

"He says horses are turning over so fast, he doesn't want to wait."

"That's right," said the third man. "He's planning to send us to Saskatoon with a few. We should be able to sell them quickly, then we'll go south and find us some more."

"You got the coffee pot on?"

"I surely do."

"Well, then, what are we doing talking out here when we could be drinking coffee in there?"

The three men laughed and walked into the shack.

"I wish Rolf would sell our oxen and buy two horses," said Erik.

"Those aren't field horses," said Colin. "I'm not even a farmer and I know that. Those horses are for riding and pulling buggies."

"Like Tapper." They both went to see Tapper whenever they could, finding him in the corral at the edge of town or sometimes in the stable at the lumberyard. Erik had ridden Tapper again a few times, always faster than he wanted to go.

Erik looked wistfully at the horses for a moment, then stood up. "We better go. It must be close to suppertime."

On the last day of June, Erik moved the manure pile from beside the chicken hutch, where he'd heaped it over the winter, to nearer the garden where it would be ready to use when rotted.

It was a breezy day, sunny but not too hot. A good day for working outside, or it would be if he didn't want to do something else. Anything else, really.

Rolf was out with the oxen breaking more land. Erik would need them to move the manure, but he thought that he and Elsa could push the empty wagon over to the pile so he could get started.

On his way to the house to get Elsa, he glanced toward the trail. A rider was approaching in a cloud of dust. Erik smiled, knowing it had to be Olaf – no one else went from one place to another that quickly.

"*Morn,* Erik," called Olaf as he turned toward the yard. "What? You aren't working?"

"Of course I'm working," said Erik. "I was waiting for you to come and help me push the wagon over here."

"What? Did those big strong oxen die?" Olaf swung off Tapper and led him into the shed.

Erik followed, protesting. "I just cleaned in here. If Tapper makes a mess you have to clean it."

"Fine, fine," said Olaf. "Now where are these dead oxen?"

Erik laughed, leading the way to the wagon. "They're not dead, Rolf is breaking land." He waved his arm to the north. "Somewhere out there."

"Ah, well, I'm as strong as an ox," said Olaf. They pushed the wagon over to the shed, then Erik offered a fork to Olaf.

"Since you're so strong, do you want to shovel manure?"

"I'll watch," said Olaf, shaking his head. "See how it's done."

"Oh, sure," said Erik, "like you've never shovelled manure."

Olaf's head suddenly jerked back, and he whipped around. "Did you hear something?" he said. "I'll be in the shed with Tapper. I'll keep him quiet. Don't tell anyone I'm here."

"Who? What?" stammered Erik, wondering if he was worried about Rolf coming back. Then he saw three horsemen approaching the yard.

Mystified, Erik stood still as the men rode up to him. Olaf's friend Jim stayed on his horse, watching Erik's every move. The other two, Pete from the livery stable and a man with a droopy moustache and bushy eyebrows, dismounted, ground tying their horses where they stood.

"We're looking for Olaf Hanson," said Pete. There was no friendliness in his voice. "Where is he?"

What should he say? Olaf didn't want them to know he was there. All Erik's English left him.

"What's the matter?" the other man growled. Erik stared at him, realizing he'd seen him before, not just at the livery stable, but in Hanley. "Can't you understand English? Stupid Norwegian," he said without waiting for an answer. "Just like his cousin."

"Olaf," said Pete with exaggerated emphasis. "We want Olaf."

Erik shrugged his shoulders. "I don't know where he is," he said in Norwegian. He shook his head, then added in English. "Not know where Olaf." If they said he was a stupid Norwegian, thought Erik, he'd act like a stupid Norwegian.

He stuck his fork into the manure pile and tossed a forkful into the wagon. He hoped they wouldn't see his hands shaking. He had no idea why they wanted Olaf, but it couldn't be good, not from the expressions on their faces. Not from the way Olaf hid when he saw them coming.

The men stepped closer, Pete pressing in on one side of him, the man with the black moustache on the other.

"When you see Olaf, tell him Pete's looking for him. Can you remember that? *Pete.*"

"He'll remember," said the other man. His words sent a shiver down Erik's back. Erik swallowed hard and nodded. The man grabbed the fork from Erik's unresisting hands and stabbed it deep into the pile. "Won't you?" he asked, his face so close Erik could smell his breath.

The men went back to their horses and mounted. Erik didn't move, watching as they rode back to the trail.

"They're gone," he said when they were out of sight. He pulled the fork out of the pile and turned toward the shed.

Olaf stepped into the doorway.

"Why do they want you?" asked Erik. "I thought you were friends."

"So did I," said Olaf. His voice was hoarse and he cleared his throat. "I mean, Jim and I were friends, but lately..." His voice trailed away. "Something's wrong. I don't know what."

Erik looked at Olaf's face and wondered if that was true.

"Who were those men?" Erik and Olaf swung around as Elsa came running from the house. "I saw them talking to you and I was too scared to come outside."

"No one," said Olaf, "I mean, no one you should be scared of."

"They wanted to know the way to...Hanley," said Erik at the same moment.

"I'm glad they're not going to Green Valley," said Elsa. "I didn't like them at all."

"Tapper likes your shed," Olaf said, changing the subject. "Can I leave him here overnight?"

"Sure," said Erik, making no attempt to hide his surprise. "But you'll have to walk to town."

"I'll get him in the morning," Olaf said. "I'm riding in the races tomorrow at the celebration."

"He'll win for sure!" said Erik. "I can't wait to see him beat the others!"

Olaf smiled, but Erik thought he still looked worried.

"Here, let me help you with that."

Olaf took Erik's fork and furiously forked manure into the wagon, not stopping till his shirt was wet and sweat ran down his face.

CHAPTER NINETEEN

Celebration

When Rolf returned to the yard, he tethered the oxen, then went to the house. "Can supper wait a few minutes?" he asked.

Inga came to the door, holding Leif, with Elsa close behind her. Erik paused beside them, setting a pail of water on the ground.

"Look at our wheat and oats!" said Rolf, waving his arms. "You can almost see the plants grow."

Rolf took Leif in one arm and put his other around Inga. They walked across the yard, with Erik and Elsa following.

Rolf led them right into the field. The grassy, green plants brushed their legs as they walked, reaching Erik's knees. The field was bright green, much greener than the prairie around them. Maybe Rolf wasn't such a bad farmer, after all.

"It looks like a beautiful crop, Rolf," said Inga.

"We have so much to be grateful for," said Rolf.

"Ja," said Erik. "The well."

"And the calves," added Inga.

"Baby Leif," said Elsa.

"The trees," said Rolf.

"Rhubarb turnovers," said Elsa. "From our own rhubarb plants."

Rolf ruffled Elsa's hair. "Especially the rhubarb plants!" he agreed.

"The whole farm is growing," said Inga. She took Leif from Rolf, giving him a little bounce so he laughed and waved his fists.

"Just like my family," added Rolf. "Not so long ago I was alone, and now, look at us all!" He reached out, resting a hand on Erik's shoulder, his other arm circled around Inga to reach Elsa.

Rolf's hand felt warm and comfortable. Erik glanced at Rolf's smiling face. Maybe even a thirteen-year-old needed a father, he thought, if the father was someone like Rolf.

"And tomorrow we'll go to Green Valley to celebrate," said Rolf. "They're expecting hundreds of people to come for the day."

"Hundreds!" exclaimed Elsa. "I still don't know why they're coming to Green Valley."

"They want to see the town that grew so quickly," said Rolf. "Most towns would take years to get where Green Valley is now."

"Can we eat the rhubarb turnovers now?" asked Erik.

"We sure can," said Inga, "but first we'll have fish."

The next morning, Erik woke in the sun-warmed tent knowing it was going to be a special day. He heard a horse whinny and sat up. He'd forgotten about Tapper. Quickly pulling on his clothes, he crawled out of the tent and looked around.

Olaf, walking briskly, was almost to the yard. Turning his head, Erik saw Rolf step out of the house, the milk pail in his hand.

"I thought I'd get the milking done before you got up," said Rolf, grinning at Erik.

"I can do it now," said Erik. He took the pail from Rolf and watched as Rolf saw Olaf.

"You get up early," said Olaf, looking at Rolf.

"Good morning, Olaf," said Rolf. "You get up even earlier." He cleared his throat. "I'm surprised to see you walking."

A whinny from the shed drew all eyes in that direction.

"Tapper?" said Rolf.

"Yes," said Olaf. "I needed a place for him for the night."

There was a pause. Erik knew that Rolf would see through that. Lars had a stable that was much more convenient than this one.

"Is there a problem?" asked Rolf.

"No," said Olaf. "No problem." He opened the shed door. A moment later he came out with Tapper and the saddle.

Rolf got a pail of water from the well, bringing it to Tapper as Olaf saddled him.

"*Takk,*" said Olaf.

"If you need help," said Rolf, "you only have to tell me."

"Everything is good," said Olaf.

Rolf's face showed his doubt. "If you say so," he said slowly. "You should know." They watched Tapper drain the pail.

"Thank you again for the well," said Rolf. "I shall always be grateful for that."

Erik saw Olaf lift his eyes and look at Rolf for a long moment.

"You're welcome," said Olaf at last. "I'm glad the water is good."

He swung himself into the saddle and whirled Tapper around.

Rolf picked up the water pail and went back to the well. Erik shook himself and headed for the shed to milk Tess.

Rolf and Olaf had spoken to each other! This day was turning out more special than he'd expected. Of course, Olaf had lied, but it was a start.

When Erik brought the milk into the house, he was greeted with the smell of cooking meat.

"What is that great smell?" asked Rolf, coming in right behind Erik.

Inga looked up from dishing out porridge and smiled.

"Chicken!" Elsa announced joyfully. She tucked a towel over a bulging basket. "We didn't tell you, but yesterday Mama and I killed a chicken and today she fried it, and we'll have it for dinner."

Rolf shot a surprised look at Inga.

"It had a bad wing," she said. "And this spring's chicks are half grown already. I thought we could spare one hen for such a special day."

"But how can we eat breakfast while we smell the chicken?" asked Erik, sitting down on the bench. "We should eat it right now!"

"You have to wait," retorted Elsa. "But I tasted it. Mama let me have the back."

"The back doesn't have any meat on it anyway," said Erik.

"Does so!"

"Erik! Elsa!" Rolf's voice cut through their argument. "I'm sure we'll all enjoy the chicken. At noon."

Erik bent his head over his bowl, ignoring the little smile Elsa gave him.

The streets of Green Valley were lined with vehicles when the oxen and wagon drove into town. Most were horse-drawn, but there were automobiles, too. More wagons, buggies and carts were near the sports grounds with their horses tied to them. When they parked their wagon there, Erik could see only one other pair of oxen.

"We'll all meet back here for our picnic before the horse races," said Inga.

She handed Leif to Elsa, then climbed down from the wagon, careful not to catch her Sunday dress. Erik tied the oxen to the side of the wagon, then carried them each a pail of water.

"Can I come with you, Erik?" asked Elsa.

"Doesn't Ma want you to help with Leif?"

"She's going to Aunt Kirsten's," she said. "I don't want to sit around the house all day. I want to be part of the picnic."

"You can help her find her friends from school," said his mother. "I don't want her wandering alone with so many people in town."

Rolf pulled out his pocket watch. "I must go. I'll try to be here for dinner, but I can't promise."

Rolf had a job for the day. He and eight other men had been hired as temporary policemen to help keep order along with the Royal Northwest Mounted Police from Hanley.

Erik and Elsa walked with their mother to the lean-to behind the store, where Kirsten and Lars were still living while their house was being built. The streets were full of people, all dressed in their best for the Dominion Day celebration.

When their mother and Leif went inside, Erik and Elsa stood on the sidewalk and looked around.

"Where shall we go first?" asked Elsa.

Before Erik could answer, he heard the whistle of an approaching train.

"To the station," he said. "Let's watch the passengers get off, then look for Sara."

They hurried down the street and around the corner, dodging through the crowds. They arrived at the train station just as the train pulled to a stop. Hundreds of people streamed out when the doors opened.

Some of the passengers carried bats and baseball gloves. Others were dressed in fancy clothes, the ladies holding sunshades.

"I thought you would be here," said Colin, popping up beside Erik. "Did you ever see so many people?"

"Only in New York City when we came to America," said Erik. After the last person stepped off the train, they went to Sara's house. Leaving Elsa there, Erik and Colin went to the sports grounds where they watched football and baseball by turns.

He met with the rest of the family for their chicken dinner at the wagon, then Erik went back to the race-track. The crowds seemed even bigger than in the morning. Erik watched the runners for the first race assemble, choosing the third from the end as his favourite. A white horse with black markings, he looked strong and fast.

Not as fast as some of the others, though, because he placed third.

Colin's choice was even worse than Erik's, coming in dead last.

When the next group of horses lined up, Tapper was on the outside edge, with Olaf sitting easily on his back.

"There's Olaf," exclaimed Colin. "I bet he wins."

"He will for sure," said Erik. "Tapper is the fastest horse ever!"

The horses pranced impatiently, waiting for the race to start. There was some kind of delay and the roar of the audience grew louder. Finally the race began. Tapper was the leader from the first moment. Behind him, Erik heard a man exclaim, "I've seen that horse before."

"Which horse?" asked his companion.

"The dark bay," he said. "The one in the lead. He

won races all over Montana last summer; I'm sure it's the same horse. He looks the same when he runs, with his tail arched like that."

Tapper made running look fun. He and Olaf crossed the finish line more than a length ahead of any of the others. After Olaf received his ribbon and prize envelope, Erik ran over to congratulate him.

"Did you win money?" he asked.

"I think so." Olaf opened his envelope and looked inside. "Five dollars," he said.

"That's great!" exclaimed Erik, remembering he'd pitched sheaves for ten days to make five dollars. "Are you racing again?"

"*Ja,*" said Olaf. He ran his hand over the horse's heaving side. "We'll be in the final race to see which horse is fastest of all."

"That's the one with the fifty-dollar prize," said Colin.

"Fifty dollars!" exclaimed Erik. "That's more money than you can make in a month."

"Or two months," agreed Olaf. "But we haven't won it yet." He led Tapper away a couple of steps.

"Hey, wait," said Erik. "I just remembered. A man said he knew Tapper. That he won races all over Montana last summer."

"If he was a prize winner, Pete couldn't have bought him for a livery horse," said Olaf. "They're mistaken. He's an ordinary looking horse."

"All except his scars," said Erik. "They don't look ordinary at all."

"You can't see them much when he's wearing the

saddle," said Olaf. "You've healed well, haven't you, old boy?"

"Let's go back to the races," said Colin.

"Sure," said Erik. "We'll be cheering for you when you race again."

Olaf smiled briefly over his shoulder. Erik watched them go, the Bar C on Tapper's hip moving with each step he took. Turning back to Colin, his eye caught someone familiar in the crowd, also watching Olaf. It was Jim, and the dark man with the long moustache. Erik saw them speaking, their heads close together, then he lost them in the crowd.

Erik returned to the track with Colin, but it was hard to pay attention. He was afraid for Olaf, but what could Pete's men do in a crowd like this? Even so, he would warn Olaf the next time he saw him.

The winner of each heat earned a spot in the final race with Tapper. After a palomino won the last race, Erik sighed with relief.

"Olaf's horse can beat him, easy," he said.

"Some of the others will be harder," said Colin. Erik nodded, but he was confident Tapper was the fastest.

They crossed the racetrack and watched baseball for a while, then moved down to the football field.

"It must be nearly time for the final race," said Erik. "I wonder where Olaf is."

"He's probably getting ready," said Colin.

"Let's see if he needs any help," suggested Erik.

They met Rolf as they pushed through the crowds. "Have you seen Olaf?" Erik asked.

"Right after his race," said Rolf, "but not since then."

"His horse is the fastest horse here," said Colin.

"We'll find out soon," said Rolf. "I thought you boys would be watching the ball games."

"We're going to help Olaf get ready," said Erik.

Rolf raised his eyebrows. "What help does he need?"

"We'll brush Tapper," said Colin.

"And tie flowers in his mane," added Erik.

They laughed and left Rolf. Erik expected to find Tapper in the corral on the edge of town, but he wasn't there.

They turned toward the lumberyard, meeting Elsa and Sara along the way.

Surprisingly, Tapper wasn't in the stable, and the house was empty. "We must have just missed him," said Colin. "He's probably already back at the racetrack."

Erik nodded, but didn't agree. It was easy to miss a person in these crowds, but a horse?

Although it was the middle of the afternoon, there were lineups at the hotels and the restaurants. Close to the race-track, people milled around a food booth in a huge tent.

"I'm hungry," said Elsa. "We still have turnovers in the basket."

"Sounds good to me," said Colin.

As they neared the wagon, Erik saw Tapper tied next to the oxen. He shot a surprised look at Colin, but Colin was already looking for a brush for Tapper's coat.

Elsa dug the food basket out from under the wagon and handed out turnovers and cookies. Erik carried some water to the oxen and Tapper, then had a drink himself.

"Is it time for the race?" asked Elsa.

"It must be close," said Erik. Olaf was still nowhere in sight. Erik followed the others back to the racetrack, his eyes moving from person to person, looking for Olaf.

There was a backwards race in progress amid loud laughter from the crowds, but near the starting line, Erik saw the winners of the main races start to gather.

Where was Olaf?

He wasn't going to pass up an opportunity to win fifty dollars. There had to be a reason why he wasn't there, and Erik feared the reason was Pete.

"Colin." Erik nudged his friend. "Stay here with the girls. I'm going back to the wagon."

"They'll be fine," said Colin. "I'll come with you."

Erik shrugged, then quickly told Elsa what they were doing. "Stay here till after Olaf's race," he said.

Elsa's attention was on the horses struggling to finish the race backwards. "Yes, yes," she said. "Look at them! Oh, no. Someone fell off."

Erik and Colin ran back to the wagon, hoping they'd find Olaf saddling Tapper. When he wasn't there, Erik grabbed the saddle and threw it onto Tapper's back.

"I'll see if he's at the livery stable," said Colin. "They might have been playing cards and didn't realize how late it was."

Erik paused in the middle of tightening the cinch. "I don't think he'll be there," he said. "Pete is angry at him about something."

"I'll take a look anyway," said Colin.

"If you want," said Erik. "But don't ask for Olaf by name. And be careful."

"I'm not worried. I've been there many times."

Erik untied Tapper. "Come on, boy," he said. "You've got to race. If we can find Olaf, that is. I doubt they let horses run without a rider."

A ladies' race was in progress when Erik arrived at the track, but his relief was short-lived. As soon as the winner was announced, they called for the final race.

Erik led Tapper over to the starting line. The palomino, a black horse with white stockings, and another bay were already there. Other horses joined them as Erik scanned the crowd for Olaf.

"You can beat them all, can't you, boy?" Erik whispered to Tapper.

"Hanson?" asked a man Erik didn't know. "Tapper?"

"Yes, sir."

"Fourth position," said the man.

"Now?" asked Erik.

"Better now than after the race." The man moved on, consulting a book in his hand.

Erik led Tapper over to the fourth position.

"You riding that horse, boy?" asked the man on a big grey beside him.

"I don't know," said Erik. "I – I don't think so."

"Well, you'd better figure it out soon," said another man. Erik saw the pistol in his hand and realized he was the starter. "We're going to start right away. Mount up."

Erik took one last look around. He couldn't see any of his family. He was alone in a sea of people he didn't know.

CHAPTER TWENTY

Pete

Erik put one foot in the stirrup and pulled himself onto Tapper's back. "Can you do it for me, Tapper?" he whispered. Tapper's ear twitched and Erik took it for agreement.

Erik scanned the crowd again, still hoping to see Olaf. Maybe he went to get Tapper, found him gone and was looking for him. He'd be angry, and Erik didn't blame him.

How had he got himself into this mess?

The ball games were halted for this last race, and people crowded both sides of the track. The bleachers were filled to capacity. Erik couldn't see Olaf in the crowd, but if he was there, he couldn't miss Erik at the starting line.

The starter pistol went off with a bang. The horses burst onto the track, Tapper taking off with the rest, not waiting for a signal from Erik.

Erik clutched the reins with one hand, Tapper's mane with the other. He should have shortened the stirrups, he realized, almost panicking. He clung to Tapper's sides with his knees, and bent over his neck.

There were horses in front of him, horses behind, horses on each side. There were only eight in the race, weren't there? There seemed to be more.

But fear wouldn't win the fifty dollars for Olaf. Erik tried to think. He'd watched Olaf in the first race. Tapper needed to be on the inside of the track, but there were horses in the way, running just as fast as Tapper.

Or maybe not quite as fast. The grey dropped behind, replaced by the palomino. Its rider was beside Erik, then the horse's head was level with him. And the bay? He couldn't see it anywhere. A black with white stockings was leading. Could he guide Tapper ahead of the palomino at his side?

The race was only a half mile, with no time to think.

Erik gave a sideways tug on the reins, then realized Tapper had already moved. He was on the inside now, going around the curve. They were coming up behind the black horse. Erik hung on tight, letting Tapper run the race his own way.

"Good boy," he shouted, though he knew Tapper couldn't hear him for the pounding hooves and yelling crowd.

The man on the black horse used his whip, and the space between the two horses grew. Erik stretched low over Tapper's neck, feeling his stride lengthen. Tapper was closing the gap.

There was no gap!

Erik could have touched the black horse, they were so close, squeezed into a space Erik hadn't known was there, on the inside of the track. Erik was even with the rider on the black. The horses were neck and neck.

Out of the corner of his eye, Erik saw the flag marking the finish line flash past. He glanced to his right where the black horse thundered beside him, his rider pulling on the reins. The crowd cheered louder than before, but Erik couldn't tell who had won.

He straightened up, tugging on the reins. They were at the next curve before Erik could get Tapper slowed enough to turn around.

The black horse with the white socks pranced beside a circle of men in suits while one of them handed his rider a white envelope. They must have won, thought Erik. But the men still stood there, looking at Erik. Was there a prize for second place, too? Maybe there'd still be something to give Olaf. Would it matter that he wasn't the right rider?

"Congratulations, young man." Erik could barely hear the man over the cheers of the crowd. "That horse of yours surely can run."

"And you are quite the jockey," said a man beside him.

Erik listened in a daze as one of the men made a short speech, then handed him an envelope and a red ribbon. Erik clutched them in his hand, nodding speechlessly.

A red ribbon! Tapper had won! They'd won the race!

"I must take care of Tapper," he finally got out. *"Manga takk.* Many thanks."

The cheers of the crowd died away as Erik dismounted and led Tapper off the track.

"Erik!" exclaimed Elsa, appearing at his side with Sara. "You won, you won!" She took the ribbon from Erik's unresisting hand.

"Tapper won. I didn't know what to do." He took the ribbon back and tucked it with the envelope in the pocket of his trousers. "Do you know where Olaf is?"

"I didn't see him," said Colin. "The door to the livery stable was closed, and barred on the inside."

"Barred?" repeated Erik. "That doesn't make sense." He looked at the horse breathing heavily beside him. "I need to tend to Tapper. We have to think."

They walked Tapper back to the wagon where Erik tied him again. Working together, they rubbed the horse down, then gave him some water. Afterwards, Erik turned to Elsa. "You should go to Aunt Kirsten's. Ma will be there. I'm going to look for Olaf."

Elsa set her face. "I'm coming, too."

"Not this time," said Erik. He and Colin strode off quickly, leaving Elsa and Sara behind. Looking back, he saw Elsa by the wagon, glaring after him. When he checked again, the girls were nowhere in sight. Erik breathed a sigh of relief. He didn't want Elsa mixed up with Pete and his gang.

Despite the crowds watching the ball games, the streets were still full of people. Erik and Colin hurried as best they could, looking for familiar faces.

When they reached the livery stable, the wide front doors were closed, just as Colin had said. "We could go 'round back," suggested Colin.

"What's the matter," demanded a voice behind them. "Why's the door shut? It's not cold out."

Erik turned to see a tall, broad man in work-stained clothes.

"It's closed," said Colin helpfully.

"Not for long it isn't," said the man. "I want my horse right now." He grabbed the handle of the wide door and gave it a hard pull. The door rattled but didn't move.

"Hey, Pete!" the man yelled. Erik stepped back, out of the way. "What's going on here? Open the door."

They heard the sound of metal on metal, then the big door started to slide.

"Hi there, Rob." Pete appeared briefly before stepping back to open the door further. "Hope we didn't keep you waiting too long."

Erik quickly stepped inside the dim stable, Colin right behind him. He saw Pete look at them, his mouth hard.

"Jim," he yelled. "Show these boys the way out, will you?"

Erik glanced around, seeing Jim coming toward him from the back of the stable. He headed toward him, vaguely aware that Rob was already leading his horse outside.

"Have you seen Olaf?" Erik asked. Jim looked at him strangely, as if he didn't understand. Erik knew his English wasn't great, but not that bad. "Olaf," he repeated. "Have you seen Olaf?"

Erik heard a muffled sound from the back of the stable. He pushed past Jim, rushing down the alley. Behind him, he heard Colin yell. Erik's eyes darted from side to side, glancing into each stall. In the last one he saw Olaf against the back wall, bound and gagged.

"Olaf!" Erik grabbed at the gag, but the knots were too tight. He felt in his trousers for his pocket knife and cut the gag loose. "What's going on? What happened?"

As he reached for Olaf's wrists, he heard a scuffle and Colin stumbled into the stall, with Pete and Jim right behind. Pete lunged toward Erik, but Colin threw himself in front of Pete, tripping him.

Erik quickly sliced through the ropes on Olaf's wrists and bent toward his ankles, but Pete saw what he was doing. Jumping to his feet, he swung at Erik's arm, knocking the knife from his hand.

Colin reached for the knife, but Jim shoved him from behind, sending him sprawling across Olaf's legs. Olaf leaned sideways and swept the knife up, just before Pete could kick it out of the way.

Erik dived toward Pete, trying to knock him down, but tripped over Colin. Swinging around, Pete grabbed Erik by the shoulders and slammed him against the wall of the stall. Erik slid to the floor, dazed, barely seeing Olaf slice through the ropes around his ankles.

A second later, Jim pushed Colin down beside Erik just as Olaf sprang to his feet. He stood, poised to move, one hand rubbing the red marks on his face, the other clutching Erik's knife. Jim and Pete blocked the entrance to the stall.

Pete shot Erik a quick look. "Nice of you to drop by," he said, breathing heavily. "Now you can persuade this stubborn cousin of yours to tell us where he keeps that horse."

"Horse?" said Erik. "Why do you want his horse?"

"Because he's mine." Pete stood in the doorway of the stall, his eyes on Olaf. Erik looked at Jim, hoping to see a spark of friendship, but his face was unreadable.

"You gave Tapper to Olaf because he was almost dead. Olaf took care of him and nursed him."

"I don't mind giving away a dead horse," said Pete. "But not a prizewinning racehorse, especially one wearing that brand."

Brand? Prizewinning? But if Pete knew Tapper had won the prize, he'd know where Tapper was. Then Erik remembered the man who said he'd seen Tapper race in Montana.

Someone rattled the door. Pete must have closed it again after Rob left.

"Get rid of whoever's there, will you, Jim?" said Pete. "Don't let them in. Lead their horses outside."

"Sure thing." Jim turned and walked away. Erik looked at Pete standing alone in the doorway. If they were going to get out of there, it had to be now.

Olaf had the same thought. He lunged forward and threw himself at Pete, missing him when Pete stepped sideways. Erik jumped up to help Olaf, but before he had a chance, Pete threw a vicious fist into Olaf's face and another into his stomach. Blood spurted from Olaf's nose as he fell against the wall.

Erik met Colin's eyes, then jerked his head at Pete. At the same moment they sprang forward. Pete's right fist came up, but Erik grabbed his arm, hanging on with all his weight. Pete twisted toward Erik as Colin took hold of his other arm.

Pete roared in rage, shaking both his arms, almost lifting Erik off the ground. A second later, Erik felt Pete going down. Olaf had scrambled behind them and pulled

Pete's legs out from under him.

Erik dropped to the floor, too, still holding Pete's arm. He pressed Pete's face to the floor with his knee, then tugged his arm over to meet the one Colin was holding.

Pete yelled and struggled to escape but Olaf was already winding a rope around his wrists, the same rope that had held Olaf earlier. Erik and Colin both slid onto Pete's back. Pete didn't give up. He twisted and turned beneath them, swearing furiously.

Erik shot a quick glance over his shoulder. What was Jim doing? They needed to move quickly in case he was getting more of Pete's men.

Olaf picked up another rope and, with blood still running from his nose, tied Pete's ankles.

"What's going on?" Rolf suddenly appeared in the doorway to the stall, with Jim beside him. Light in the alley told Erik the big door was open again.

"Rolf!" exclaimed Erik. "I'm so glad to see you." Then he saw Elsa, right behind Jim.

"I got him for you," she said, catching Erik's eye. "When that man locked you in the stable, I knew it was a bad thing, so Sara and I found Papa."

"I don't know what's happening," said Erik. "We came in here and found Olaf tied and gagged, so we let him go, and then we…"

"Tied up Pete?" said Rolf, his voice dry.

Erik nodded.

Rolf pulled a handkerchief out of his pocket and handed it to Olaf. "Why did he tie you up?" asked Rolf,

"Did he hit you, too?"

"Ja," said Olaf, wiping the blood from his face. "When Pete gave Tapper to me, he didn't really own him. He was stolen, and now he wants him back."

Erik gasped, but Rolf didn't look surprised. He looked at Pete, still on the floor. "Is this true?"

Erik felt Pete stiffen beneath him, but he didn't answer.

"It's time for the police," said Rolf. Erik was looking at Jim while Rolf spoke, and saw his face turn white. He turned to leave.

"Jim!" yelled Erik. "Don't go. You're part of this, too."

Rolf stepped back, one arm coming out and stopping Jim in his tracks. "Maybe you stay here till it's all sorted out, *ja?"*

Rolf pushed Jim into the stall with the rest of them. "Elsa, you and Sara find one of the Mounted Police and bring them back. We'll wait here."

"What about Pete?" said Jim. "Can I untie him?"

"The boys can get off," said Rolf, "but leave the ropes till the police come."

When the Mounted Police constable arrived, Olaf told about being captured by Pete and Jim. Each of the others told their part, except Pete who refused to speak. Jim, watching Pete, said very little.

"There's another man, too," said Erik suddenly. "Dark, with a big moustache. He was at our place yesterday, looking for Olaf, along with Jim and Pete."

Rolf shot him a surprised look.

The policeman listened to Erik's story, then turned to

Olaf. "This horse of yours, the one that Pete gave you, does it have a brand?"

"Y-yes," said Olaf hesitantly. He looked down at the floor for a moment. "It's a Bar C."

"Mmhmm. And do you know who put that brand on the horse?"

"No, sir. Many of the horses had the same brand."

"Seems a whole herd of Bar C horses were stolen last summer from a ranch in Montana," said the police officer.

"I learned today that Tapper was stolen," said Olaf, "but I should have guessed before. This friend of Pete's used to come to a corral north of town. No one was supposed to talk about him. He covered brands with other brands, mostly the Boxed Q."

The policeman nodded. "Based on what I've heard," he said to Olaf, "I won't take you with me, but we'll continue our inquiries. Don't go too far away." He looked at Rolf. "Can I depend on you to make sure he's here when we need to talk to him?"

Rolf looked at Olaf, one eyebrow lifted. Erik held his breath.

Olaf nodded.

"You can," said Rolf. "I will be responsible for my son."

Erik let his breath out.

The policeman handcuffed Jim and Pete and took them away. Colin and Sara went home right afterwards. Rolf looked at Erik, Elsa and Olaf. "We've spent enough time in this stable. Let's go."

Suddenly Erik remembered the race. "Olaf," he

exclaimed. "I almost forgot. When you weren't around, I brought Tapper to the racetrack so he'd be ready for you. And when you didn't show up," he paused and looked at Olaf. He couldn't read anything in his face. "I...I rode him."

He dug in his pocket and pulled out the ribbon and the envelope.

Olaf glanced at his outstretched hand. "You won?" he exclaimed. "You rode Tapper in the final race, and you won?"

"No," said Erik. "*I* didn't win. I just hung on. Tapper ran the race all by himself."

Everyone laughed.

"So take the money," said Erik. "It's yours. If you have to give Tapper back, at least you'll have some money to buy a new horse."

"It's yours," said Olaf. "You won." Then he grinned. "I mean, you rode in the race."

"Yeah," said Erik, "but I only did it for you." He walked over to Olaf and shoved the envelope and ribbon into his hand, closing his fingers over them. "And every minute I wished you were there."

"He might not have won if I'd ridden him," said Olaf, opening the envelope. "I weigh more than you."

Erik stood by Olaf, watching as he pulled a wad of bills out of the envelope. They counted them together. Ten five-dollar bills.

"It's possible," said Rolf slowly, "that the real owner of the horse should have the money."

"But Olaf cured him," protested Erik. "If he hadn't, Tapper would be dead."

Olaf put the money back in the envelope. "I guess we'll wait and see," he said, "but if we don't have to give it away, it's yours."

"Papa, I almost forgot," exclaimed Elsa. "Aunt Kirsten is making supper for all of us. I saw her when I was looking for the policeman."

"Then we should head that way," said Rolf.

"Right now!" Elsa started for the doorway. "I'm starving."

"I'm ready, too." Olaf looked at Rolf for a long moment, then added, "Father."

Rolf dropped his arm around Olaf's shoulder. They stepped out of the stall behind Elsa, then Rolf glanced back.

"Are you coming, Erik?"

Rolf gestured toward Elsa running out of the stable into the sunshine. "It's a wide door," he said. "Wide enough for me *and* my sons."

"I'm coming, Pa," said Erik. "Don't you worry about me."

Acknowledgements

Racing Home is fiction but, like all historical fiction, it grew out of reality. In this case, I was inspired by the development of the town of Outlook, Saskatchewan. Like Green Valley, Outlook is situated southwest of Hanley on the South Saskatchewan River near a valley of American Elms. The auction of the lots, the swift building of the businesses, the arrival of the train, and the July 1 celebration are all part of Outlook's history. Most of this I learned from *Milestones and Memories 1900 to 1980,* the community history book of Outlook and surrounding area. I am grateful to the compilers for their diligence in keeping our past from being forgotten. The rest of the story is a product of my imagination, and in no way reflects the real people or events in the history of Outlook, or any other town.

Thank you to Barbara Sapergia for her help in the development of this book. Without her insight, guidance, and encouragement, *Racing Home* would never have made it around the final curve.

About the Author

Adele Dueck has published three other books for children. *Nettie's Journey, Anywhere but Here* and *The New Calf.* Before turning to writing for children, she wrote for magazines and newspapers, mostly about the humorous side of rural living.

Born in Outlook, Saskatchewan, Adele lived in Drake, Lanigan and Saskatoon before moving to Lucky Lake, where she farms with her family.

ENVIRONMENTAL BENEFITS STATEMENT

By printing this book on FSC-certified recycled paper,
COTEAU BOOKS
ensured the following saving:

Fully grown trees	Litres of water	Kg of solid waste	Kg of greenhouse gases
8.06	29 712	450.06	1 169.88

These calculations are based on indications provided by the various paper manufacturers.

Manufactured at Imprimerie Gauvin
www.gauvin.ca

RECYCLED
Paper made from recycled material
FSC® C100212